BUCKSKIN CROSSING

BUCKSKIN CROSSING

A Novel by

ROBERT CALLIS

iUniverse LLC
Bloomington

Buckskin Crossing

iUniverse books may be ordered through booksellers or by contacting:

iUniverse LLC
1663 Liberty Drive
Bloomington, IN 47403
www.iuniverse.com
1-800-Authors (1-800-288-4677)

ISBN: 978-1-4917-0443-1 (sc)
ISBN: 978-1-4917-0444-8 (ebk)

Printed in the United States of America

iUniverse rev. date: 08/22/2013

DEDICATION

This book is dedicated to my wife, Nancy L. Callis. A retired English teacher, she has been my proof reader, editor, and full time critic. The smartest thing I ever did was marry her.

PROLOGUE

OCTOBER 17, 1928

A thick fog hung over the Rock Springs, Wyoming, airfield like some giant cobweb whose shape continuously changed as the slight wind that ebbed and flowed from the west seemed to push it back and forth.

The light spilling from the front door of the small office of the U.S. Air Mail Service was suddenly broken into several shadows as a stocky figure clad in a bulky winter flight suit stepped out of the cramped office and into the cold, foggy night. He was medium height, and he sported a five day growth of beard on his face. He stood briefly under the small overhang which was providing minimum shelter from the elements and paused to light a cigarette with his Zippo lighter. He paused and held the Zippo up to the light and read the inscription "Wild Bill." He smiled and pocketed the lighter. He then blew out a stream of cigarette smoke, which quickly gained altitude as though trying to join forces with its smoke-like fog brethren.

William "Wild Bill" Hopper was a professional airplane pilot. He had served in the Army Air Corps in France in World War I. After the war he was hired by the U.S. Postal Service as a pilot when they initiated carrying the mail by airplane or Air Mail in 1920.

Bill had held on to that job, sometimes by the skin of his teeth, for eight years. Wild Bill was a free spirit and he had a penchant for experimenting when he was flying. Once he interrupted a mail flight to land in a field next to a county fair because he wanted a cup of coffee. He managed to keep his job because he was one of the best pilots the Post Office had, and he never missed work.

In 1928 Congress decided to get the Post Office out of the aviation business and passed a bill to provide putting up for bid contracts to provide air transportation for the mail of the U.S. Post Office. The bidding was done by newly formed independent airline companies.

Bill was suddenly out of a job as the contracts were awarded, and the Post Office shut down their aviation program. He was quickly hired as a pilot by one of the new airlines National Air Transport, which had been awarded the contract to carry mail by air between Omaha, Nebraska and San Francisco, California, and back. This was the fourth leg of the transcontinental air mail route. The contract required both daytime and night flights.

Night flying was more dangerous and pilots who flew at night were paid more. Bill had opted for the better pay of $2,800 a year and flew at night almost exclusively. Night flights had been introduced only after several improvements had been made. The first improvement was the use of radios. Between Omaha and San Francisco were several stops including North Platt, Nebraska; Cheyenne, Rawlins and Rock Springs, Wyoming; Salt Lake City, Utah; and Elko and Reno, Nevada. Each of these stations had a radio with the exception of Rawlins, Wyoming. The radio provided weather information for the pilots.

The second improvement was the establishment of a system of beacon lights along the air routes. These beacon lights could be seen from ten miles away on a clear night. They were, in effect, small lighthouses for the air mail pilots.

Bill tossed his unfinished cigarette into a nearby puddle and watched as it hissed, smoked, and then went silent.

He was not happy with the weather report he had just received from the Rock Springs office radio. A storm was moving across the Rocky Mountains and was likely to make his trip from Rock Springs to Salt Lake City a rough and bumpy ride.

After a pause to look up at the night sky, the pilot started walking out to his airplane, the front of his unzipped flight suit flopping back and forth as he walked onto the tarmac where his plane, a DeHaviland 4B, was parked. He passed a small building where the grounds crew had set up an empty fifty-five gallon barrel and one of them was tossing chunks of wood and some greasy rags into the fire.

Bill ignored the improvised warming station and walked directly to where his aircraft was parked. He then slowly walked around his airplane, pausing to carefully check several key components as he made his circle.

The DeHaviland was a more recent model of the plane that was flown in World War I. The plane had two open cockpits, one in the front and one behind it. The plane had been re-designed so the pilot sat in the rear cockpit and controlled the aircraft. The front cockpit was modified to hold a waterproof container holding approximately five hundred pounds of mail.

The Liberty 12 engine in Bill's airplane had been built by Ford Motor Company in 1922 and had a top speed of 115 miles per hour. It had a reputation of landing hard at a high speed and so engineers added reinforced landing gear and a larger elevator. The DH was considered a good plane for mountain flying with its large wingspan. The DeHaviland was also considered quite reliable in all kinds of weather.

Bill had finished his inspection trip around the aircraft and was about to light another cigarette when the door to the U.S. Mail office opened and the interior light from the office cascaded out into the surrounding darkness.

Two mail clerks came out pulling a small four-wheeled cart and headed for Bill's aircraft.

The two clerks pulled the cart over to Bill's aircraft and began loading mail packets into the front cockpit container. When they were finished, one clerk pulled the cart back to the office and the other came over to Bill holding a clipboard.

"Hey, Wild Bill," said the clerk.

"Hey, yourself Wally. What's the scheduled load for tonight?"

"Well, we got approximately four hundred and eighty-nine pounds of packet mail," replied Wally.

"How come there's less than five hundred pounds?" asked Bill.

"We was told to leave space for a special eleven pound packet, which ain't showed up yet."

"Shit," responded Bill. He was anxious to take off and try to get through the mountains before the expected storm. Any kind of delay could be trouble.

"Well, if it ain't here, I ain't signin' for it," snarled Bill as he pointed at the clipboard Wally was holding.

"Take it easy, Bill. You know I don't make the rules."

Bill glared at Wally and then turned to spit into the darkness. "This is government bullshit."

Wally said nothing, and he slowly backed away from the angry pilot. He had seen examples of Bill's temper before and wanted no part of being on the receiving end.

The door to the office opened again and released the pent up light that seemed to be stored behind it as it spilled out into the fog where it was quickly swallowed up. Two men in trench coats and snap brim hats exited the office and headed toward Bill and Wally. One of the men was tall and thin, and the other was short and stocky. To Bill they seemed to remind him of some cartoon characters he had seen somewhere in his past.

The two men stopped in front of Bill and Wally. The tall one spoke. His voice was soft, but firm. "Are you Mr. Hopper?"

Bill looked at him and nodded yes.

"Very well then," he said. He pulled out a piece of paper and handed it to Bill.

"This should complete the transaction, Mr. Hopper."

Bill took the clipboard and pencil from Wally and tried to read the detail on the paper. The only thing written was "Ten pounds of mail in a one pound metal container."

"What the hell is this?" exclaimed a very angry Bill.

Without even looking at Bill, the short man stepped between Bill and the tall man. The tall man seemed to float backwards, away from Bill. The short man whispered something to the tall man and then turned to Bill.

He reached under his trench coat and pulled out a small locked box made of light weight metal locked with a small, but stout looking padlock. He then handed the box to Wally who looked at it and handed it to Bill.

Bill turned the box over in his hands and examined the metal box and its padlock.

"OK, I give up, what's in the box?"

Both of the men were silent.

"Look boys, I'm not signing for something I don't know about, and if I don't' sign, the package don't go. You boys understand?"

The two men looked puzzled and the tall one looked angry. The short man turned and again whispered something in the ear of the taller man.

The tall man looked at Bill with a face full of exasperation and obvious dislike.

Before the tall man could speak, the short man pushed his companion aside, stepped forward, and confronted Wild Bill.

"This package is to be delivered to the International Diamond Exchange in San Francisco by tomorrow morning. It contains ten pounds of cut and finished diamonds.

You are to tell no one and I mean no one you are carrying these diamonds. That includes the ground crews in Salt Lake, Nevada, or San Francisco. Do you understand what I have just told you, Mr. Hopper?"

Bill was taken by surprise by the short man's strong outburst. "Yes, I understand," Bill replied.

"Good. If you are now satisfied, I suggest you get underway as quickly as possible."

Bill grunted and nodded his head in acknowledgement and turned to Wally and grabbed the clipboard from him. Bill signed the clipboard, handed it back to Wally and walked to his airplane. After the packet was added to mail container in the front cockpit and the container sealed by Wally, Bill stepped up on the wing and slid into the cockpit. Once he was properly seated and belted in, he turned to look back at the two strangers. All he could see was fog. They were gone.

Five minutes later, Bill was airborne and headed west toward Salt Lake City.

Twenty minutes into the flight, it became more difficult to keep the light beacons in sight. The fog made it difficult to see the beacons and the wind became stronger and made it more difficult to maintain his course. The fog was so thick it was difficult for Bill to see his meager set of instruments, particularly his compass.

The winds had shifted and seemed to be coming from the southwest and were getting stronger by the minute. Minutes later the fog was now accompanied by snow and gusting wind pockets began buffeting the aircraft.

Bill knew he had to be careful. If he dropped down in altitude to try to get a better chance to see the light beacons, he would take the chance of hitting a mountain top. He had to keep his altitude and try to ride out the storm.

Almost an hour later, he knew he was fighting a losing battle. The snow had now turned to a form of sleet and Bill was sure his wings were icing up, as his controls were getting more and more sluggish. If the wings got iced, over he would lose control of the aircraft and it would drop out of the sky like a rock.

The controls had become even more sluggish, and Bill knew he was losing altitude. He decided his best chance was to drop down and try to find a place to land. Once on the ground he could wait out the storm. He tried his radio, but all he could get was static. He sent out a mayday call and gave the current time, but he had no idea of his location. The plane was becoming very difficult to control. It was taking all of his strength to just move the control stick and pedals.

Bill slowly and carefully pushed forward on the control stick and the aircraft slowly responded and began to dive down to a lower altitude.

'So far, so good," thought Bill.

He remembered he had emergency lights under the airplane to help in a landing like this one so he found the switch and turned them on.

All at once the wind seemed to blow the aircraft sideways and Bill and the airplane were out from under the fog. He could now see fairly well. He tried to level out the aircraft and was struggling to pull back on the control stick when he realized he was flying next to a mountain peak, towering above him to his right. He could see what looked like some kind of sloping snow field below him. He slowed down his airspeed and steered the aircraft to the center of the snow field. Bill slowly brought the aircraft down and lessened his speed. Bill could see he was coming to the end of a fairly long snow field. He began a sharp turn to the left and held tight on a shuddering stick until he had reversed his flight and was headed back where he came over the snow field.

As he got closer to the snow field, Bill cut the power to the engine to try a dead stick landing. It wasn't ideal, but the last thing he wanted was a fire. The white snow field was rushing up at him, and he prayed it was only snow and not a field of boulders covered with snow. The aircraft pancaked onto the snow field, bounced twice and then pancaked again and everything went black.

CHAPTER ONE

SUBLETTE
COUNTY
WYOMING

THE PRESENT

Lew Cavanagh pulled back on his reins and brought his mare to a halt. He slowly dismounted and tied the mare off to a large clump of sagebrush. Lew spread his legs and bent forward at the waist to stretch the stiff muscles in his lower back. Lew was sore from two straight days of tracking four wayward cows and their calves.

He had been riding since dawn, and he had camped on the banks of Dutch Joe Creek the previous night. His tall lanky frame was looking forward to a real bed instead of the cold, hard prairie ground. He was also looking forward to a solid hot meal that included more than coffee, beans, and bacon.

Satisfied that his back was as good as it was probably going to get he stood upright, stretched all his back muscles and walked over to his horse. He reached into his saddlebags and withdrew his old and slightly battered field glasses. After pulling his field glasses up to his eyes, he adjusted them and slowly scanned the base of the mountain to his east and the narrow box canyon to his north. He was slightly east of

Sagebrush Ridge and about four miles from the west edge of the Wind River Mountains. The east fork of Squaw Creek was about two hundred yards to his east.

The creek flow was headed south, running down from its origins in the mountains to his north and east.

The Wind River Mountains ran about ninety miles from the north end to the southern tip. Lew was slightly north of the south end of the mountain range. The scenery around him had changed radically in the past three hours. Sagebrush and rock that had been his constant companion for two days had been replaced by small lakes and ponds, lots of green grass and plenty of pine and quaking aspen trees.

"Amazing what a little snowmelt water will do," he thought.

Lew was forty-nine years old, and he had been a cowboy ever since he was old enough to ride a horse. He had tried his hand at several jobs, including the rodeo circuit, but he wasn't good enough for real prize money and he hated working indoors.

He sat down on a large rock and took off his dusty cowboy hat and set it on the rock with the brim up. Cowboy legend had it if you placed your hat with the brim up, none of the good luck in the hat would spill out. Lew didn't figure he could afford to lose any of the good luck the hat might still possess. He brushed his sparse blonde hair back on his head and pulled a battered hard pack of Marlboro's out of his shirt pocket.

He pulled his lighter out of his jean jacket pocket and lit a cigarette. He inhaled and felt the smoke flow through his system. He could almost feel the relaxing effect on his body. Even his back seemed a little better.

Lew looked up at the mountains to his right. "Pay might not be much, but this view beats the hell out of any office I ever saw," he thought to himself.

Lew had been a ranch hand for the Wine Glass Ranch for the past six years. During the winter he worked as a line rider, checking on the cattle scattered along the west slope of the Wind River Mountain Range. During the summer months, he worked on the ranch with the other hands.

The Wine Glass Ranch was a good outfit, as ranch outfits went. It was owned by some rich folks from the East who probably only spent a few weeks each year during the summer living at the ranch. The owners were smart enough to hire a top hand like Luke Code to run the ranch. Lew worked for Luke and he liked him. Luke was fair and he worked just as hard as any of the ranch hands. He never asked them to do something he wouldn't do himself.

Lew had spent the past four weeks rounding up stray cows and their spring calves he found on his assigned portion of the western part of the ranch. As he collected the cows, he placed them in a fenced box canyon while he left to search for other strays. When he was done he would ride to the main ranch house and get help to move his herd back to the main herd, unless help had already arrived at the box canyon.

Lew was pretty sure he was almost done. These last four cows had been hard to find and even harder to track. He was confident he would find them today now that he was up against the west slope of the Wind River Mountains. Those cows had finally run themselves out of real estate. Lew would be happy to be done. He was looking forward to a warm, dry bunkhouse, plenty of hot food, and a chance to go to town and have a few beers.

His break over, Lew put out his cigarette by crushing it on the rocks with his boot. He mounted the mare and

3

continued to track the wayward band of cattle, noting that the tracks were following along the banks of Squaw Creek heading toward the lower reaches of a mountain to his west, but at a slightly northern angle. As he got within a half mile of the beginnings of the rising rocky side of the base of the mountain, Lew paused and pulled out his field glasses again. This time he scanned the rocky slopes to the north and the beginning of the downward sloping snow field that began about one hundred yards up from the rocky base.

As he scanned the terrain, he saw something out of place and he stopped scanning. He refocused the field glasses and sure enough, there, up on the top edge of the rocky rise just below the snow field, was his long lost little cattle herd.

Lew smiled to himself as he moved the mare to a trot to get close to the cows as quickly as he could without alarming them. As he got to within fifty yards, he slowed the mare to a walk and angled his approach to slightly west of the cows, making sure he could cut off that route of escape.

The cows and calves were drinking from a small pond of water created from the run-off of the melting snow field. They looked up as he approached, but did not make any indication that they might be inclined to try to escape.

Lew let out a sigh of relief. The long chase was finally over. Apparently one of the calves thought otherwise as she suddenly bolted away from the herd to the west and at full tilt.

"Crap," said Lew as he put his heels to the mare's flanks and took off in pursuit.

After a chase of about a hundred yards, the snow under the fleeing calf gave way and she tumbled head over heels finally sliding to a stop in the soft snow.

Lew brought the mare to a halt next to the downed calf and quickly dismounted and pulled the calf to her feet. He inspected the trembling calf and found nothing injured. He picked up the calf turned her towards her mother and gave her a swat on the rump. The calf took off running toward the rest of the cows bawling loudly as she ran.

Lew watched her go and he smiled to himself. As he turned to grab the mare's reins, he saw something dark and shiny by his boot half-buried in the snow. He knelt down and dug away about five inches of snow and carefully pulled the object out of the confining snow field. He brushed off the snow and slowly turned the eighteen inch dark metal cylinder over in his hands. He could see a symbol stamped in top and bottom of the metal side. It looked like the word "Liberty" and he thought he could see small things like wings on either side of the L.

Lew wrapped the cylinder in a rag he had and placed the wrapped bundle in his saddle bag.

Lew stepped away from his mare and looked up at the sun. He still had plenty of daylight to get the small herd back to his box canyon corral.

Lew made good time although he did have a little trouble with the herd, but it was almost dark by the time Lew was able to drive them all the way to the box canyon corral. He was pleased to see there were many more cattle in the corral than when he left two days ago.

As Lew and his herd approached the gate, a figure in a cowboy hat stepped out of the surrounding dusk and opened the gate to let the cattle into the corral.

"Where the hell did you go to find this mangy bunch of dumb cows?" asked the figure.

Lew grinned at Curly Polk's wise ass remark. "Same place they're keeping the hair that's supposed to be on that cue ball of a head you got, Curly."

Curly Polk had gotten the nickname because he had been bald since he was sixteen years old. Lew never failed to remind him of it.

Curly was short and thin with a wiry build. He was younger than Lew, but not by much. They had known each other for over twenty years.

After all the cattle had filed into the corral, Curly closed the gate and gestured to a small campfire he had built about forty yards away where three large rocks formed a natural shelter from the wind.

After Lew had removed the saddle from his mare, he used the saddle blanket to wipe off and then rub down the mare's back. Lew put a set of hobbles on the mare's forelegs and then slipped a crude oat-filled feed bag made out of burlap over the mare's head. Curley brought over a bucket of water and placed it within reach of both Lew's mare and his own horse, who was hobbled nearby. The two cowboys sat on the ground next to the small campfire and drank coffee out of battered tin cups.

"What's on the menu for tonight?" asked Lew."

"Well, we got a new shipment of beans and bacon along with somthin' extra," said a grinning Curly.

"Extra?"

"Yep, shot me a prairie chicken and got her roasting on a spit over the fire."

Lew looked at the fire and sure enough, there was the prairie chicken on a spit with a pan underneath on the coals to catch the drippin's. Another small pan with a lid was full of bubbling beans and a small black skillet sat on a nearby rock with bacon slices spread out, ready to be fried.

After the two cowboys had polished off their dinner and washed their utensils in the nearby creek, they sat down by the fire to have a final cup of coffee.

Curly looked over at Lew and said, "It sure would be nice to have something to spice up this coffee. You know, like a dessert."

Lew got the hint and stiffly stood up and walked over to his saddle and opened up his saddle bag for the metal flask of whiskey he was known keep handy. As he found the flask, he remembered the metal cylinder and pulled it out as well.

As Lew rejoined Curly by the camp fire he tossed him the metal cylinder. "Found this in a snow field where I found the cattle. Ever seen one before?"

Curly smiled and said, "Does it have whiskey in it?" Lew snorted in reply. Then Curly looked at the cylinder turning it over in his hands. "Nope, can't say I ever did. What the hell is it?"

"I don't rightly know, but I'm fixin' to find out."

"How the hell did it get up here in a mountain snow field?"

"Maybe it's from outer space. Maybe it belonged to some alien who crashed into the mountain?"

"More likely it fell off of some kind of airplane, if you was to ask me"

"Well I did ask you and you don't know nothin' more about it than I do."

Curly looked the cylinder over carefully and then handed it back to Lew.

"Where the hell did you say you found this thing, Lew?"

"I didn't say nothin' about where I found it, Curly. But since you asked, I found it in a snowfield about fifty yards in from the south edge."

"South edge? South edge of what?"

"The south edge of the snow field, you dummy."

"So now I'm a dummy, huh? Well last time I was dumb enough to chase lost stock up into the Wind Rivers there was a damn ton of snow fields along with lakes and ponds and even some pretty damn huge glaciers."

Lew felt himself blushing at Curly's retort. Curly was right, there were lots of snowfields in the Wind River Mountain Range.

"Actually, this here snow field was just north of the head of the lower fork of Squaw Creek."

"Squaw Creek! I recollect there is five fingers off that creek near its head."

"Yep. That's the one. This was the finger that runs most to the north and if you was standing where I was and you was to look up, you'd be lookin' at the north end of Knife's Edge Glacier."

"Knife's Edge? Ain't it the high narrow glacier at the very top of the south end of the Wind Rivers?"

"The very same," replied Lew.

"Wonder if there might be more stuff up near where you found this cylinder thing?"

"I didn't see nothin' but this here piece."

Curly reached over and tossed a couple of pieces of firewood on the camp fire.

"That ought to keep the chill off," said Curly.

After adding some whisky to their coffee, Lew replaced the flask and the cylinder in his saddle bags. The cowboys finished their coffee and slid into their bedrolls, using their saddles for pillows. Pretty soon the loudest sound in the prairie night was their snoring.

CHAPTER TWO

Four days later, Lew and Curly and the rest of the ranch hands were finished with the round-up and headed for the bunkhouse to shower and change clothes for a trip into town.

Town was a relative term. The short version was Buckskin Crossing which consisted of a single commercial enterprise the Buckskin Mercantile and Bar, which sold everything from western clothes, horse tack, hardware, ammunition, and gasoline plus almost everything you would find in a gasoline convenience store. The kitchen consisted of a small stove and a microwave, but the bar served beer and whiskey. Buckskin Crossing was only twelve miles from the ranch, but the road was rutted and often muddy.

Buckskin Crossing was actually a ford of the Big Sandy River. Sometime in the 1860's a trapper and hunter named Buckskin Joe lived there with his wife and daughter. The crossing was used by trappers and fur traders in the early 1800's. Captain Bonneville and later John C. Fremont and Kit Carson used the crossing. This ford of the Big Sandy River on the Lander Cut-off of the Oregon Trail was heavily used by west-ward bound emigrants. Hundreds of emigrant wagons and thousands of their livestock used this crossing on their way west. This was the mail route from the east to the west side of the Wind River Mountains in the early 1900's. Now it was home to a ramshackle road house that served as a mercantile and bar.

The long version was the town of Pinedale, a small town of about 2,000 people with bars, stores, and motels. Pinedale was also about 42 miles from the ranch on slightly better, but not much, roads.

If your goal was to get stinking drunk, then Buckskin Crossing was just fine. The trip was shorter and there was little chance you would get arrested for drunkenness and tossed in jail. There was no local law enforcement unless a county deputy or a game warden happened to be in town, and there was no jail.

Pinedale was a whole different story. Pinedale attracted a lot of tourists on their way to Yellowstone National Park and the town's fathers were careful to see they did not get disturbed by the local riff-raff. Getting drunk in Pinedale could be both problematic and expensive.

Lew, Curly, and four other Wine Glass Ranch hands settled for Buckskin Crossing.

Curly drove his battered old Ford pickup truck. Curly, Lew, and Andy were crowded into the front of the ancient truck and Squirt had squeezed his small body into the tiny bench seat in the back of the cab. Rusty Dawkins and Vince Owens sat on a hay bale and hung on for dear life in the truck's bed. It took them almost fifty bump-filled minutes to finally arrive in Buckskin Crossing. Curly pulled off the bridge over the Big Sandy River and down the gravel covered grade to where the Buckskin Crossing Mercantile and Bar was located and lurched to a halt. Everyone piled out of the pickup and headed into the bar. Lew had held back, and Curly turned to see what was holding him up.

"What the hell are you waitin' for? The beer ain't gonna get no colder?"

"I'll be right with you, I got some business in the mercantile first," replied Lew.

As the noisy group of cowboys disappeared into the door to the bar, Lew reached under the seat and took out the cylinder he had found and wrapped in a relatively clean rag. He carried his bundle in one hand and entered the door to the mercantile.

Frosty Stubbs, the owner of the Buckskin Crossing Mercantile was behind the counter, reading a newspaper he had spread out in front of him. Frosty was mostly bald with a thick growth of pure white hair on the sides and back of his head. He was a short and portly man shaped like a pear. He was always dressed with a white shirt and bib overalls. Sometimes the white shirt was clean and sometimes it wasn't. Tonight it was clean.

"Hey, Frosty, what's up?"

"It sure as hell ain't my dick, Lew. How are things with you?"

Frosty's wife had left him and run off with some hippies five years ago, and he was still pissed about it. Since his wife had left Buckskin Crossing, no white woman had been in the place.

Lew strode up to the counter and carefully laid his bundle down in front of Frosty.

"It ain't my birthday," said Frosty, "so what the hell is this you brung with you?"

"I found it up in the mountains during our round-up, and I ain't rightly sure what it is."

"Well, let's have a look at it," said Frosty.

Lew pulled away the rag covering the cylinder and handed the cylinder to Frosty. Frosty turned it over in his hands and then set it down on the counter.

"Let me get my readin' glasses on, and we'll see what we got here."

Frosty donned his reading glasses and slowly turned the cylinder, stopping several times to study it.

"Do you know what these markings are or what they mean?" asked Frosty.

"I got no idea," said Lew.

"So what you gonna do with it?"

"I thought I'd try and sell it and get a little beer money out of it," replied Lew.

"Hmmm," said Frosty as he continued to study the cylinder. Finally he placed the cylinder on the counter and looked up at Lew.

"How much you want for it?" asked Frosty.

Lew paused to think. He hadn't really thought this far ahead, but a little cash was worth more to him than a metal cylinder he had no practical use for.

"How about a hundred bucks?"

"A hundred bucks! What are you anyway, a crazy person. You don't know what it is and I don't know what it is, and it may be worth something or it may be worth nothing. I'll take a chance and give you forty bucks for it, take it or leave it."

Lew thought for a minute and then looked down at Frosty and said, "Deal," and stuck out his hand. Frosty shook hands on the deal and then popped open the old fashioned cash register and counted out four ten dollar bills.

Lew took the bills and stuffed them in his jeans pocket. He thanked Frosty and walked to the side entrance to the bar.

Frosty rewrapped the cylinder in the rags and placed the cylinder under the counter and turned to his little desk behind the counter. After getting seated on his swivel chair, he booted up his desktop computer and waited to get access to the internet.

"OK baby, let's find out what we got here."

CHAPTER THREE

An hour and a half later Frosty sat back in his chair in disgust. He could find nothing that looked like the metal cylinder he had just purchased from Lew. He had searched surplus airplane parts sites and historic airplane sites and he was still stumped.

He took the rags off the cylinder and carefully looked it over for the tenth time. He studied the image stamped on the end of the cylinder and on impulse he went to Google on the computer and typed in "Liberty".

In a flash Frosty was looking at the image of a Dehaviland 4B two-seat biplane. After reading about the aircraft on several sites including wikipedia, Frosty slowly realized his mistake. The image stamped on the cylinder was the name of the engine, not the airplane.

Frosty found a schematic drawing of the airplane and after blowing up the size of the images in the schematic, he identified what he had in front of him. The cylinder was the distributor for a Liberty 12 engine used in the DeHaviland DH4B. A little more reading and he discovered that the plane and engine were likely used by the Air Mail Service in the 1920's.

Now that he knew what he had, Frosty began searching for what the distributor might be worth. By searching several antique airplane parts sites, he came up with some examples and he sent out several e-mails to the sites inquiring about selling the distributor.

Frosty looked at his watch and was surprised to see that almost three hours had gone by since he first started his internet search. He shut off the computer and stood up from his chair. He stretched his arms and back to try to get the stiffness out. What he needed was a beer, he decided, and Frosty headed for the adjacent room that contained his bar.

Frosty spent a couple of hours in the bar. He split his time between helping his bartender Skinny serve drinks and tossing down a few drinks with his customers. All of his customers were local cowboys, and he knew all of them pretty well. Frosty was a bit of a skinflint who was unlikely to offer anyone, no matter whom, a free drink. Frosty also had a softer side and kept a couple of cots in a back room where a cowboy could sleep off a drunk and not get in any trouble.

Frosty made it a point not to cheat anyone and did so because he depended on the repeat business of the cowboys. His establishment got a lot more trade in the summer from backpackers, hunters and fishermen, but in the winter, it was strictly the local cowboys he depended on for their business.

By the time he and Skinny had served a last round and herded the drunken cowboys outside so they could close up, it was about two o'clock in the morning.

Frosty half-stumbled up the stairs to his apartment on the second floor, and Skinny made his way to his little camper trailer parked behind the Mercantile.

Just before he slipped into bed, Frosty remembered the emails he had sent out about the distributor. He reminded himself to check the computer in the morning to see if anyone had responded to his inquiry. As he fell fast asleep, he doubted anyone was awake and looking at emails inquiring about the value of a ninety year old airplane distributor.

CHAPTER FOUR

Frosty awoke the next morning to the sound of slamming doors and boots on the wooden floor below him. As he rolled out of bed, he realized the noise was coming from Skinny and some delivery guy who was making his Saturday morning stop to replenish Frosty's beer supply.

Frosty tossed on some clothes and hurried downstairs to help with the delivery and make sure he was getting every last beer he was paying for.

After they were done, Frosty paid the driver from the invoice and went back into the kitchen located behind the bar. There Skinny was making breakfast for both of them. Eggs were cooking on the stove and bacon sizzled on a cast iron black skillet that was older than Frosty.

After they finished eating breakfast, Frosty took a cup of coffee with him as he went back into the Mercantile and sat at his desk behind the counter. He noted on his desk calendar that beer was the only delivery scheduled for this Saturday and then he remembered his emails from the night before.

Frosty opened up his computer and signed on to the internet and was stunned to see he had fifteen emails from the night before. Who writes e-mails late on Friday night, he wondered. He noted one of the e-mails had been sent at two o'clock in the morning.

He opened the first email. It was from one of the antique airplane parts sites he had sent an inquiry to the night before.

The email sender noted that the part might be worth up to $100 depending on the condition and he was prepared to offer $50 sight unseen.

"That don't smell right," said Frosty to himself.

Sure enough, each of the emails gave different values, but all of them had cash offers for the distributor sight unseen.

Frosty smiled. All these emails told him the distributer was worth a lot more than $100. Maybe even more than $1000. Frosty knew the best way to get the highest price was to put the distributor for sale on eBay. He could do that and let each of the email senders know what he had done, so they could duke it out and Frosty would be the beneficiary.

A quick check of his notebook told him what his password and member name were for eBay and he carefully wrote out his description of the distributor to have the maximum effect. Then Frosty got out his small digital camera and took a couple of pictures of the distributor including one that caught the "Liberty" imprint.

As he composed his ad, Frosty decided that he would put a $1,000 minimum reserve on the distributer and then he entered the text and the photos to his eBay account. As he finished with his ad and watched his photos flying into the internet, he smiled and rubbed his hands together. Frosty loved making a profit.

Frosty was correct that those web sites he had contacted would duke it out on eBay for the distributor after he failed to take their initial low ball offers. By the end of the week that his ad was supposed to run on eBay, the ad had collected over 2,000 hits and the bidding had run up to $1,850.

Frosty was ecstatic.

Unbeknownst to Frosty some of the people who were among the 2,000 hits were not actually interested in buying the old airplane distributor. Their interest was in the actual plane and its cargo.

CHAPTER
FIVE

Several months had passed since Frosty's great eBay auction success. He had received a last second bid for $2,000 from a buyer in Pennsylvania and after he received the money he had shipped the old aircraft distributer by Federal Express to its new owner. Frosty had been so overcome by his good fortune that he had actually given Lew Cavanaugh an extra twenty dollars which Lew promptly spent in the Buckskin Crossing Mercantile and Bar.

Spring had replaced winter around Buckskin Crossing and the melting snows turned lousy roads into really muddy and almost impassable roads. Frosty stood on the front porch of his mercantile building and looked across the landscape with a hot cup of coffee in his hands. He knew that spring was a very short season in the mountains of Wyoming and that things would get very dry very quickly.

Frosty had not been entirely generous in offering Lew an extra twenty bucks. He had tried to get Lew to go back to the snowfield where he found the distributor and see if there was anything else of value that Frosty could sell on the internet. Lew had shown no interest and when Frosty had tried to get the location of the snow field, Lew had clammed up and refused to talk about it. Finally, Frosty had given up.

As Frosty drained his coffee cup he thought to himself that sooner or later Lew would need some beer money and he would make a second trip up into the Wind River

Mountains and search out the snow field where he had found the distributor. Frosty tossed the remnants of his coffee over the porch railing and headed back into the mercantile.

*   *   *

Lew had given some thought to Frosty's idea of going back to the snow field and looking for other items from what was the wreckage of an old airplane that had flown and crashed long before Lew was even born. He had decided that he would return to the site, but he was not telling anyone about it, not even Curly and certainly not Frosty. He knew Frosty had made a lot of money off the distributor and he would either get a better deal from Frosty from any future items or he would find a way to sell them on the internet for himself. Lew was not sure what else might be found at the snow field, but he knew he would have to be careful so no one followed him there or whatever was buried in the snow field would soon disappear from his reach.

CHAPTER SIX

"Kit" Carson Andrews walked slowly along the bank of the narrow creek, his eyes searching the clear rushing waters for any sign of trout. The sun was high in the clear blue sky and there was almost no wind. He stopped and stood motionless while he looked and listened and smelled his surroundings. He detected nothing except for a light wind in the leaves of the quaking aspen in a small grove behind him and in the small willow trees that sporadically lined the creek bank.

Andrews was a tall young man with wide shoulders and an athletic build. He wore cowboy boots, jeans and denim shirt and a well-worn black cowboy hat. He wore a fishing vest and a back pack with a small hand net attached to the side and he carried a well-used fly fishing rod in his right hand. All in all, he looked like a typical western fly fisherman. The difference came with a bulge under the left side of his fishing vest. Strapped to his chest, invisible unless you were looking for it, was a leather shoulder holster housing a Kimber .45 caliber semi-automatic pistol.

He continued his slow journey along the creek until he found what he was looking for. The creek dropped about two feet and created a pool of water about ten feet across and about three feet deep.

He adjusted his hat and unlimbered his fly rod. He whipped the rod back and forth several times and then he cast his bait, a wet fly, onto the surface of the creek, just above where the water dropped into the pool.

The fly landed neatly in the middle of the creek and then began to flow down-stream with the current until it dropped over the edge and down into the waiting pool. Just as it floated out into the pool, the fly disappeared in the mouth of a cut throat trout. Kit expertly flicked his rod up and knew he had hooked the trout. He quickly reeled in the trout and after a short but physical effort by the trout to pull free, he had the trout in his net. He took the hook and bait out of the fish's mouth and put the fish on his stringer. Then he attached the end of the stringer to a small willow tree and dropped the rest of it including the trout into the cool waters of the pool.

Kit stood and again he remained silent and unmoving as he watched, listened to and smelled his surroundings. Satisfied that he was still alone, he checked his bait. He noticed the fly was a little the worse for wear after it's encounter with the trout, so he decided to replace his lure.

Kit found a flat rock under one of the quaking aspen trees and sat in the welcome shade to begin changing his bait. Andrews had just finished tying a new wet fly to his line when he felt a vibration and then he heard a familiar sound. He stood up and turned to face the source of the growing noise.

Directly in front of him, he saw his best friend Swifty Olson on horseback moving quickly across the buffalo grass and sagebrush dotted plain that led up to the small creek.

Kit carefully laid his fly rod on the ground next to a nearby willow tree and waited for his friend to pull up and dismount.

"At least all the fish in this creek are safe with a duffer like you on the other end of that fly rod," said Swifty as he tied his horse off to a small stand of mesquite.

Kit laughed and stepped forward to shake hands with his old friend. "What in the heck would drag you away from a good card game in the Stock Exchange Bar on a Saturday afternoon?" asked Andrews.

Swifty was a tall lean man with ropey muscles and a very confident smile. Like Kit, his skin was darkened by the sun and he was dressed in dusty denims, his curly brown hair covered by a sweat-stained cowboy hat that was once cream colored and a pair of worn and scuffed cowboy boots. He wore a look of confidence and the former Delta Force operator oozed a sense that could best be described as cocky. Swifty Olson feared no man and just a few women including his mother.

"You wouldn't happen to have anything decent to drink would you partner?"

"Define decent."

"How about something that will clean the dust out of my throat and could be used for snakebite medicine in a pinch."

Kit walked over to the small creek and pulled on a small rope that was tied off to a small willow tree. The other end of the rope was in the creek. Kit soon pulled up a small wire basket with four cans of beer in it. He opened the wire basket and took out two cans, tossing one to Swifty and dropping the basket back into the creek.

The two friends sat on the flat rock under the large willow tree in the shade and opened their beers. Swifty finished his beer in about three swallows and motioned with his hand for the beer that Kit was still holding.

"Good lord, you're supposed to drink them, not inhale them" said Kit as he tossed his beer to Swifty and shook his head at his friend while he proceeded to get another beer from the basket.

Swifty finished off his second beer, gave a loud belch, and tossed the empty beer can on the ground.

"Is there a reason for this special visit or were you just thirsty and too broke to buy your own beer?"

Swifty smiled. He had a dazzling smile that was quite disarming. He used the same smile on young ladies he was trying to impress and enemies he was about to dispatch.

"Actually I was sent on this errand by Woodrow Harrison, attorney at law."

"What the heck is up with Woody?"

"It seems someone has come looking for you and after a long and fruitless search has ended up in Mr. Harrison's law office."

Kit finished his beer and tossed the can on the ground joining Swifty's two empties. He took off his hat and ran his fingers back through his hair and then resettled the hat on a slightly altered landscape.

"So far I have heard nothing compelling enough for me to leave a perfectly good fishing hole and head back into Kemmerer."

"Good fishing hole? Looks to me like the only thing in your holding tank is cans of beer. I ain't seen no fish, although personally I am more partial to beer than I am to fish."

"Well, I got to assume that Woody thought this was pretty important or he wouldn't have sent your scrawny ass out to find me."

"I'll ignore that ignorant remark about my ass since I just smoked you for two free beers."

"I left my truck in the shade of some willows about a mile south of here. I'll see you back in Kemmerer."

"I'll be in the Stock Exchange Bar trying to recoup my losses."

"Recouping your losses could take weeks."

"That's very funny. Let me know what old Woody is up to and who this is that needs to find you. It's probably somebody from the government or some old relative looking for money."

With that Swifty had untied his horse and had vaulted up into the saddle and horse and rider were splashing across the creek almost in one swift motion.

*   *   *

Kit watched his friend ride out of sight and then proceeded to collect his fishing gear. When he had everything assembled, he shouldered his gear and then stood still for a moment using his eyes, ears and nose to once again check out his surroundings. This was a habit born of desperation. Three years ago Kit had been on the run from mob killers who had a contract to kill him. They had already killed two of his friends in Chicago to keep them from testifying at the trial of two mobsters Kit and his friends had witnessed killing a man. Kit had been the last man on their list.

Kit had survived two separate groups of killers and had made strong friends in Kemmerer, Wyoming. One of those friends was Swifty, who first entered Kit's life as a bodyguard hired by his father's friends Woodley Harrison and Big Dave Carlson. They had taught him how to survive and to defend himself. One of those lessons was to constantly check on your surroundings using your sight, your hearing, and your sense of smell. Being careful had saved Kit's life at least twice.

Satisfied that he could sense no danger, Kit set out walking downstream on the banks of the little creek. The winter had been harsh, but spring had brought with it new life and rebirth of plants and animals around the flood plain of the creek.

Kit could see the tracks of mule deer and antelope in the soft earth on the bank of the creek and he could see the small game trails where wildlife moved down to the creek to drink and eat.

Pretty soon he could see his truck parked under some willow trees. The truck was his first pick-up when he came to Wyoming and he had restored it and held on to it. The truck was a green 1949 GMC three quarter ton pickup, complete with a stock rack in the bed.

Kit unlocked the truck and stowed his fishing gear in it. He swept his eyes over the truck and saw no signs of any disturbance since he parked it. He slid in behind the large old steering wheel, turned the ignition key, and the truck's ancient engine roared to life. Kit smiled and put the truck in gear for the ten mile drive back to Kemmerer.

As he drove along the gravel road he wondered just who had come looking for him.

*   *   *

Kemmerer is an old mining town located about 7,000 feet above sea level in southwestern Wyoming. Today the principal economic forces are the power plant, the coal mines and agriculture. Because of the high plains desert nature of the land, agriculture is centered in sheep and cattle.

The town is nestled in the small valley created by the Ham's fork river. When he first set eyes on Kemmerer, Kit thought it was small, gritty, and backwards. Today Kit thinks of it as home.

Barely three thousand people make up the residents of Kemmerer, and that includes the residents of the small town of Diamondville on one side of Kemmerer and the almost ghost town of Frontier on the other side. Thanks to government funding, each of the three had their own post offices.

Kit pulled out onto the highway from the gravel road on the edge of town and easily made his way to Woody's law office. Kemmerer is also unusual in that the center of town is built around a triangle instead of a square. About a third of the buildings on the triangle are bars, each with their own particular socio-economic following.

Woody's office was a small stone two story building just off the main street of town. Kit parked his truck across the road from Woody's office and headed for the front door.

As Kit started to cross the street, he saw two women exit Woody's office. He stopped to observe them. One of them was a mature woman of about fifty-five or sixty. She was well dressed and Kit was pretty sure that her auburn colored hairdo cost at least twice more than everything he was wearing. The other woman was younger, maybe about twenty five or so. She was well dressed like her older companion. She moved like an athlete or at least a tomboy. Both women swept down the sidewalk and climbed into a black Lexus sedan and quickly pulled away from Woody's office. Kit resumed his walk and three minutes later he was sitting in Woody's wood paneled office in a large over-stuffed leather chair with a cold beer in his hand. Woodley Harrison was nothing if not a great host.

Woody produced a cigar and a glass of bourbon and offered a second cigar to Kit. Kit smiled and waved off Woody's generous gesture.

"Good to see you Kit. How was the fishing?"

"Not too productive, but it was still good practice."

Woody had introduced Kit to fly fishing. When they first met Woody had been fly-fishing and had gotten treed by an angry black bear. Kit had happened along and scared the bear off. Woody was happy to be rid of the bear, but being rescued by a tenderfoot like Kit at the time was a story that was told over and over again much to Woody's embarrassment.

"Well most of the streams still have too much silt in them and it is hard for the fish to see your lure. I usually wait until the fourth of July for the streams to clear and usually have great success."

"Well, I do need the practice," said Kit.

Kit took another swallow of his cold beer while Woody took a sip of his bourbon.

Woody leaned back in his big leather chair and pointed at Kit with his cigar. "I am sorry I had to send Swifty after you and interrupt your practice, but those damn women were driving me crazy and they kept coming back. I couldn't get rid of them."

"Are you talking about those two ladies who just left your office before I walked in the door? The older one and younger one who were all duded up?"

"That would be them. God they were insistent. Reminds me of why I never married."

"Just what did they want with you that might involve me?"

"Well the whole deal seems so far-fetched that I am not sure just where to begin."

"Start anywhere you want, but I would prefer somewhere near the beginning."

"That's easier than it sounds, but here goes. I got a phone call from a woman about a month ago. Her name was Louise Stout. It seems that Ms. Stout is the granddaughter of a gentleman named William Hopper. Mr. Hopper was a pilot in the 1920's and he worked as an air mail pilot for first the government and then for a private airline who took over the air mail contract. At that time it took several legs of flying to get the mail across the country because of the size and range of the then available aircraft. Mr. Hooper flew the westward leg from Rock Springs to Salt Lake City. Are you with me so far?"

Kit nodded that he was up to speed with Woody.

"It seems that in October of 1928 Hopper left Rock Springs on a night flight headed to Salt Lake City and into an early winter storm. Hopper and his plane never arrived at Salt Lake City. Even after an extensive two week search, neither Hopper, the aircraft, or the air mail was ever found."

"Nothing was found?"

"Not a trace of the pilot, airplane, or cargo."

"And this is relevant how?"

"A few months ago some cowboy looking for a few head of lost cattle found an artifact in a snow field near the Wind River Mountain Range."

"That's a huge range and it covers a ton of miles in Wyoming."

"That is does, Kit. Anyhow, this cowboy takes the artifact to a place called Buckskin Crossing."

"Buckskin Crossing?"

"It's a spot in the road north east of Pinedale. The only thing there is the Buckskin Crossing Mercantile and Bar owned and operated by one Frosty Stubbs."

"Do you know this Mr. Stubbs?"

"Yes, I do and he is a strange, tightfisted little varmint, but he's honest. The cowboy sold the artifact to Stubbs, and he then put it on the internet and sold it to a gentleman in Pennsylvania."

"The gent in Pennsylvania is a collector of antique aircraft and parts. After he received the artifact he traced it to a DeHaviland 4B two-seater open cockpit airplane with a Liberty engine as being sold to National Air Transport

Airlines in 1927. He further traced the aircraft to the one Hopper flew out of Rock Springs in 1928."

"Wait a minute. Are you telling me this Hopper fella was flying from Rock Springs to Salt Lake City and managed to crash his plane in the Wind River Mountains? My God that's over two hundred miles north of that route."

"I said near the Wind River Mountains, not in them. I have no knowledge of the actual crash site. No one does except this cowboy who found the artifact."

Kit went over to the far wall of Woody's office where he had hung a large framed map of Wyoming with the edges of the surrounding states.

He traced a line on the map with his finger from Rock Springs to Salt Lake City. Then he took his other arm and put a finger on the Wind River Mountains.

"Do we know who this cowboy is?"

"No, we do not."

"Looking at your map this seems even more unlikely. How could a plane get that far off course?"

"Maybe his instruments failed. A winter storm could be strong winds, fog, snow, sleet, and goodness knows what else."

"What else do you know about this deal?"

"All I really know is I got phone calls, very insistent phone calls from this Stout woman asking me to put her in contact with you."

"Me, why me? What do I have to do with this deal?"

"Nothing. She found out about the artifact and she is trying to locate the crash site and the possible remains of her grandfather. She claims her family wants closure after all these years and she also wants her grandfather's name cleared."

"Cleared of what?"

"According to Ms. Stout the U.S Postal Service and the airline viewed the whole incident as suspicious and she feels her grandfather needs to be vindicated."

"OK, I buy that, but why me? Does she know me?"

"She doesn't know you, but she knows of you. She's from Charleston, South Carolina, and she read about your exploits down there last year. Somehow she sees you as her white knight."

"I don't think I want any part of this, Woody."

"Will you at least talk to her so I can get her out of my life?"

"I'll talk to her, but it will be short and sweet."

"Great, I'll call her at her motel."

"You mean right now?"

"Of course I do. The sooner the better," and Woody made the call.

Fifteen minutes later the door to Woody's law office burst open and in rushed the two women. Woody made the introductions and had everyone take a seat around his desk.

"Mr. Andrews, my daughter and I are so grateful you have agreed to help us."

"Wait a minute, Ms. Stout. I have agreed to nothing except to hear you out and then decide if I want to get involved."

"Oh, I'm sorry, I misunderstood. What do you want to know?

Kit took his time in answering her question. He studied both women who while well-dressed and well made up, had a certain hardness to them. Maybe they had a tough life, he thought. He mentally kicked himself as a reminder not to prejudge them.

"Am I correct in understanding that you want my help in finding the crash site of your grandfather's airplane in the Wind River Mountains?"

"Yes, Mr. Andrews, that is correct."

"Are you aware of what a huge area of land is involved? Do you realize that a search up there could take months, even years?"

"We know the area is large, but we felt you would be most capable as the area is in your back yard."

"With all due respect, Ms. Stout, The Wind River Mountain Range is much greater than my back yard in southwestern Wyoming. I have no experience in the terrain in and around the Wind River Mountains."

"We know this will be difficult, Mr. Andrews, but we are willing to pay you."

"Ms. Stout, this is not something that I would do for money."

"But you went to South Carolina to search for buried Confederate gold that had been hidden for over a hundred years."

"I went to South Carolina to solve a mystery observed by my deceased great-great grandfather who served in the Civil War and to find the buried bodies of five confederate soldiers who were murdered for the gold."

"I'm sorry, I meant no disrespect, Mr. Andrews."

"No offense taken, but I am not interested in your money."

"Oh!"

"Why haven't you hired a private detective or gone to the government for help in your search?"

"We have, and no one is interested because of the area."

"The area?"

"She means the fact that it's the Wind River Mountains and it's in a designated Wilderness Area. In other words no motorized vehicles," said Woody."

Kit understood. That meant searching would take place on foot or on horseback. In addition, the Wind River Mountains had areas that were impassible to even horses.

"I assume you have done some work on your own since you have come all the way out here. What have you learned, Ms. Stout?"

"We talked to a Mr. Stubbs, the owner of the Buckskin Crossing Mercantile and Bar."

"What did he have to say?"

"He told us he bought the artifact from a cowboy who stopped in his bar for a drink. He then looked it up on the internet and sold it on eBay."

"Did he tell you the name of the cowboy he bought it from?"

"No, he wouldn't tell us."

"Did he tell you anything about the cowboy, like where he worked?"

"No, he refused to talk about the cowboy."

"Does he know where the cowboy found the artifact?"

"He says he does not."

"It doesn't sound like he was very helpful."

"He was not only not helpful, he was rude."

Woody winked at Kit.

"Will you help us, Mr. Andrews?"

"I'm not sure if I can. I tell you what, I'll sleep on it tonight and I'll call you in the morning with my decision."

"Excellent," said Woody and he quickly and expertly escorted the two women out of his office.

When Woody returned to his office, he had a quizzical look on his face.

"I thought you were just going to tell them no?"

"I was, but something about this deal appeals to me. I think this Hopper guy was a tough old dude and maybe he deserves to be found and brought home after all these years."

"So you are going to help them?"

"I'm still not sure. I want to think this whole deal over tonight. There's something about those two women that bothers me and I can't figure out what it is. Something about their story just doesn't feel right."

Kit said good night to Woody and drove straight home. He made a light supper of pasta and meat sauce and had a cold beer with his dinner. He went to bed with more questions than answers.

CHAPTER SEVEN

Kit woke early the next morning and made himself a pot of coffee. While the coffee was perking, he put bacon in his large black skillet and when they were done he put them on a paper towel to drain. Then he broke two eggs into the bacon grease in the skillet.

"Don't stop there. I'd like three eggs over easy with my bacon" said Swifty who had appeared silently into Kit's kitchen.

Kit made a face and broke three more eggs into the skillet. "You'll get them hard like mine or you get zip."

Swifty held up his hands in surrender. "Okay, okay, hard it is, just like the cook."

Swifty got out plates, cups and silverware as Kit finished up with breakfast and both sat down and ate in silence.

"This is not bad for a tenderfoot like you. You might have a future as a short order cook."

"I'd starve to death with you as a customer."

Swifty laughed as he got up to refill his coffee cup.

"What did old Woodley want with you yesterday?"

"He wanted me to meet with two women from South Carolina."

"South Carolina. Did we meet them when we were down there?"

"No we didn't and they weren't here about some paternity suit so you have nothing to worry about."

"I never worry, Kit. You should know that," said a smiling Swifty.

"Believe me, there are times when you should worry. You don't even remember the names of the women you've been with."

"Why would I worry about their names? I'll never see them again."

"From their perspective, that's probably the most noble thing you do."

"Jealousy will get you nowhere. Neither will flattery. So what about these two women?"

Kit recounted his encounter with the two women the previous evening.

"So when do we start?"

"We're doing nothing. I'm still not sure about this deal and I don't trust these two females at all."

"Is it because they're females?"

"No, I have this nagging feeling about them that they're not on the up and up. Either they are not telling me the truth, or they are leaving something out."

"And so what're you gonna do?"

"Like I said, I don't trust them. But if that old Hopper guy is buried in some snowfield up in the Wind Rivers then I think it would be a righteous thing to find him and send him home to his family."

"So we're going?"

"Of course we're going. Even if I decide not to associate with these two women, there is nothing to stop two nosy guys from conducting their own search."

"Well, I better get on home and get stuff packed up. Are we taking horses?"

"Horses, a pack mule, and some cold weather gear. It may be spring, but up high, the Wind Rivers can be downright nasty. Bring Big Dave's four horse trailer on your truck with all your stuff back here, and we'll set out first thing in the morning. I need to do some searching on the internet and get some maps printed out."

Kit looked up, but Swifty was already gone.

Kit smiled and headed for his office and the computer.

An hour later, he had a pile of printed maps and detailed information about the wilderness area around the Wind River Mountains as well as the existing trails and waterways.

Kit put all the printed materials into a zip lock waterproof plastic bag and placed it on the kitchen table.

Kit then made two lists. One was for everything he needed to pack for the trip and the second list was the steps he felt they needed to follow to narrow down the search area.

Kit got up with the checklist for the trip and headed for his shop where most of the gear he needed was stored. As he walked past the locked door of his missing father's bedroom, he paused.

Reaching into his wallet he pulled out a credit card and used it to slip the lock on the bedroom door. He stepped inside and flipped on the lights. Everything was the same as the last time he had broken into his father's bedroom. The room was unchanged since the day his father had left for parts unknown and never returned. He sat on a stool in the walk in closet and tried to catch a scent of his father from the clothing hanging from rods on both sides of him. He had never known his father, as his father and mother had divorced shortly after his birth. He always thought his father was dead as that was how his mother had described him. At the back wall of the closet, hung a large framed photo montage. It was covered with photos of Kit at all stages of his life when he was growing up. He never knew his father had those photos or how he got them.

'Where was his father? Was he dead or alive? Was he rotting in some foreign prison? What had happened to him?" wondered Kit.

As he rose from the stool he brushed against a worn leather jacket and as if by instinct he pulled it to his face. He could smell a faint mixed scent of sweat, soap, and gunpowder. Kit smiled to himself. That was a combination that would never make it into an after shave. He let go of the jacket and made his way out of the bedroom, being careful to make sure the door was locked behind him.

Kit busied himself in the shop and soon had filled up his list with piles of gear and equipment. He added what he thought was an adequate amount of clothing, including cold weather gear. He packed everything into all-weather bags that could be carried by the pack horse.

When he was finished, he stacked everything on the floor of his shop. After checking his lists again, he locked up the house and drove off in his 1949 GMC pickup truck.

Once he reached Kemmerer, Kit stopped at the post office. There was no mail delivery where Kit lived so he got his mail in a post office box. The box was stuffed full of catalogs, circulars, bills, and a few envelopes.

Before he left the post office, Kit sorted through his mail and he pitched the junk mail, fliers, and most of the catalogs. As he sorted through the envelopes, a brightly colored post card slipped out and dropped to the floor.

Kit placed the rest of the mail on the counter and bent down to pick up the post card. The front of the card was a picture of an old mission in a desert setting. The caption below it said it was as mission near the Baja in Mexico. Kit turned the card over and on the front was his name and address and next to it was printed a single word. "Aloha."

Kit frowned. Aloha was Hawaiian for hello and good-bye. What did that have to do with a mission in Mexico?

He studied the writing on the front of the card. Then he smiled. He recognized the writing as the handiwork of Chris Conner. Conner was an ex-army Special Forces guy who had served under Kit's father and who had been the caretaker of his father's house when Kit showed up in Kemmerer. Conner had gone looking for Kit's father over a year before and had not returned. Then one day Conner's house was for sale and when Kit went to see what was going on he discovered that the house was empty. Conner was more like the wind than a person. He had no roots and he wanted none. The card was from Conner, but only Conner would know what the message on the card actually meant. Maybe he had gone to Hawaii. Maybe he had gone to Mexico. It was impossible to tell.

Kit walked to his truck and tossed his mail on the front seat. He started the truck, put it in gear, and proceeded to drive slowly over to Woody's law office.

*   *   *

Frosty was surprised to look out the front window and see a dark green Range Rover SUV drive up and park in front of the Buckskin Crossing Mercantile and Bar. The windows were darkened, and he could not see inside the vehicle.

After a couple of minutes, both the driver's and front seat passenger's doors opened up and two men got out of the SUV. Both men were dressed in high end clothing that Frosty usually saw on hikers and backpackers. The clothing looked stiff like it was brand new. Both men wore brightly colored tennis shoes which also looked new.

The two men soon entered the Mercantile through the front door and both stopped to look around.

"Can I help you gents?" said Frosty.

Frosty could see that one of the men was slightly shorter and thinner than the other. The larger man was bald and the shorter man had brown hair cut short. It almost looked like a military haircut.

"Perhaps you can," said the shorter man. "We're looking for a gentleman named Frosty Stubbs."

"You came to the right place. I'm Stubbs."

"Very good, Mr. Stubbs. My name is Kellogg and this is my associate, Mr. James."

"Howdy," replied Frosty. "What can I do for you?"

While Frosty and Mr. Kellogg were talking, Frosty noticed that Mr. James was walking around like he was looking for something.

"Is there something you're looking for Mr. James?" said Frosty.

James stopped and turned to look at Frosty. He smiled and moved his head side to side indicating a negative.

Frosty returned his attention to Mr. Kellogg. "Exactly why are you looking for me?"

Kellogg paused and then stepped back from the counter and pulled up a wooden chair from a nearby table and sat down. He looked up at Frosty and said, "A while ago you advertised an old airplane artifact for sale on e-bay."

"That's right. I did and I sold it. I ain't got anymore to sell."

"Actually, Mr. Stubbs, I am not interested in airplane artifacts. What I am interested in is information."

"What kind of information?"

"I'm interested in where that particular airplane artifact was found."

"I ain't got no idea of where it was found. I bought it off a cowpoke who found it while he was herdin' cattle."

"What was this cowpoke's name, Mr. Stubbs?"

Frosty felt a sudden chill in the air and he knew it wasn't from the weather. He was getting a bad feeling about Mr. Kellog and Mr. James. Mr. James was now somewhere behind him where he couldn't see him.

"I don't rightly remember."

"You don't remember the name of someone you bought an artifact from just a couple of months ago?"

Frosty did not reply.

"I don't think you're telling me the truth, Mr. Stubbs, and I dislike being lied to. So does Mr. James."

Frosty turned to see where Mr. James was and was surprised to see him leaning against the counter about five feet away and holding a gun, which he had pointed at Frosty.

"Now Mr. Stubbs, let's cut out the bullshit and get to the point. We want the name of the cowboy who found the artifact."

"Fuck you," snarled Frosty.

Mr. James had moved closer to Frosty, and he brought his gun down barrel first and caught Frosty on the side of his head. The blow knocked Frosty to the floor and the gun sight cut open a slice of his cheek and he began bleeding profusely, the bright red blood contrasting with his white hair.

"Jesus Christ. What the hell did you do that for?" moaned Frosty as he placed his hand over his bleeding wound and tried to get to his feet.

"You might want to stay down there, Mr. Stubbs, unless you are ready to tell us what we want to know."

Frosty looked up at his two assailants and then at the blood running from his face, over his hand, and dripping down on his clothes. "Fuck you."

Mr. Kellog nodded to Mr. James. Mr. James had pulled on leather gloves and he proceeded to beat a defenseless Frosty with his fists.

After almost five minutes of relentless blows from Mr. James, Frosty lay on the dirty wooden floor of the Buckskin Crossing Mercantile covered in his own blood and moaning in pain.

Mr. James pulled Frosty to his feet and sat him in a wooden arm chair where he secured his arms and legs with plastic ties.

"He's a tough little shit," said Mr. James.

"I think we can manage to speed up his cooperation," said Mr. Kellogg.

Kellog wandered down the aisles of the mercantile as though he were looking for something.

"You have a nice selection of tools Mr. Stubbs and just what I was looking for."

Kellogg returned with a hammer and a pair of channel lock pliers.

Frosty stared at Kellogg like he was crazy.

At that moment, the back door of the mercantile opened and slammed shut.

Kellog motioned to James to check it out and Frosty took his opportunity to yell out, "Skinny!"

Skinny ran through the door from the kitchen to the mercantile and James shot him in the forehead. Skinny fell to the floor and folded up like an old tent.

Frosty was shocked and unable to speak.

Kellog turned to Frosty and said, "Are you ready to tell us the name of this cowboy?"

Unable to speak, Frosty shook his head that he was not.

"Very well, Mr. Stubbs, you leave me little choice."

Kellog knelt down in front of Frosty and removed his shoes and socks.

"What the hell are you doin'," cried out Frosty.

"Mr. Stubbs, I am going to smash your toes, one at a time. Then I am going to rip them off, one at a time until you tell me what I want to know."

Frosty was horrified and terrified at the same time. He was pretty sure that no matter what he did or said, these two thugs were going to end up killing him just like they had poor Skinny.

"Well Mr. Stubbs, what is his name?"

"I don't know."

"I think you do" said Kellogg as he bought the hammer down hard on the big toe of Frosty's right foot.

Frosty screamed!

CHAPTER EIGHT

Kit stepped into Woody's office reception area and his secretary escorted him into Woody's office where he found Woody reading a fly fishing magazine.

"Kit, my boy, good to see you," said Woody.

"Good to see you too, Woody. Any word from the two ladies?"

"Oh my yes. They are waiting in my conference room where they are currently enjoying fresh coffee and some pastries and eagerly awaiting your arrival."

"Woody, I have something to show you," said Kit as he handed him the post card from Conner.

"Aloha?" What in blazes does this mean?"

"I think it's from Conner. I'm not sure what it means."

"Conner! I haven't heard from him since he sent me directions on where to wire the money from the sale of his house almost a year ago."

"Where did he have you wire the money?"

"To an account in the Cayman Islands, but I doubt that he is living there."

"With Conner, you can't ever tell for sure."

"No you can't. I think he got tired of looking for your father and then just got tired of Wyoming. He's probably someplace like Alaska."

Woody picked up a half empty coffee cup and filed it from a nearby coffee maker. "Would you like a cup of coffee?"

"No, I'm fine. Let's get this meeting with the ladies over with."

"You don't sound very enthusiastic," teased Woody.

Kit just frowned at Woody, which made the attorney laugh, and then he led the way to the conference room where the ladies were patiently waiting.

After the usual pleasantries were exchanged, Ms. Stout turned to Kit and said, "Have you made up your mind on whether to help us, Mr. Andrews?"

"Yes, Ms. Stout, I have decided to try to help you and your daughter find the crash site and the remains of your grandfather."

Both women stood and stepped forward to give Kit a hug and to thank him profusely. After a few seconds of this happy demonstration of approval, they all sat down at the conference table.

"Now, Mr. Andrews, there is the need to talk about the terms and conditions of your employment" said Ms. Stout. With that said she opened her large purse and produced a folded document of several typed pages.

"This is a contract that we have had our attorney prepare in hopes that you would agree to assist us. All we really need to do is fill in the dates and the amount of your fee."

"That's a contract?"

"Yes, that is basically what the document is," replied Ms. Stout.

Kit was silent after her answer.

He proceeded to scan through the document.

"This says that I am agreeing to a confidentiality clause that would prevent me from ever telling anyone about the location of the crash site if we were to find it?

"That is correct."

Kit frowned and said nothing.

Ms. Stout broke the ensuing silence and asked Kit, "Have you decided on a fee?"

Kit looked over at Woody for a few seconds and then turned to face Ms. Stout.

"Ms. Stout, it's my decision to help in finding the crash site and the remains of your grandfather. I believe he deserves to be found and brought back to his family for a proper burial and to give them closure."

"I'm not interested in collecting a fee nor am I interested in being paid for my services. This is the kind of a job that I undertake because I want to do it, but I agree to do it under my terms, not yours."

"What do you mean?" said Ms. Stout.

"I mean that I will seek out the crash site on my own. I will not keep silent about what I may find, nor will I conceal any details about what I find at the site. I will not take any fee nor will I sign any contract. I will share my findings with local law enforcement and your family. Beyond that I make no promises."

"You must sign the contract" said Ms. Stout. "My daughter and I plan to accompany you on the search and there will be expenses for all of the supplies for such a venture."

"Ms. Stout, I don't think you understand. I'm not for hire. I'm willing to try to find the crash site and the remains of your grandfather on my own nickel. But I will do it my way and that does not include taking a couple of greenhorn females along on a dangerous trip into the Wind River Mountains."

"This is outrageous. This is my grandfather we are talking about. Who has a better right to accompany the search for him?"

"While that may be true, Ms. Stout, none of that is my problem and I have no intention of making it my problem. I'll keep you informed of my progress to the best of my ability."

Both women sat in their chairs with shocked looks on their faces. Ms. Stout began to try to speak again, but Woody put up his hand to motion her to stop.

"Ms. Stout, Mr. Andrews has made it clear he will try to help you, but he will do it on his own and in his own way and there is nothing illegal about that. I would think you would be pleased with his offer to help, not be upset about utilizing some contract drawn up by some attorney who is not familiar to me or my client."

Without another word, both women stood and stormed out of the conference room and out of Woody's office.

"That went well," chuckled Woody.

"You can laugh about it. You don't have two crazy women trying to tie you into some goofy contract."

"I'm an attorney. We make contracts, we don't sign them."

"They seemed a little more than just upset with me."

"They'll get over it. Beside, you agreed to do what they want, just not the way they wanted you to do it."

"They must be out of their minds if they think any sane man would allow them to go along on a trip to the Wind River Mountains up on the glaciers."

"They're women. Thinking and using logic and reason don't register with them. They want what they want, period."

"I have enough trouble with Swifty, let alone some greenhorn females."

"Well, relax. They're not going. I think it wouldn't have hurt to have them pick up part of your expenses on this trip, I guess that is something that's up to you."

"This is going to be my trip where I make the decisions and I decide what is ok and what is not. I have no problem spending my money doing something that I think is the right thing to do."

Woody just smiled.

CHAPTER
NINE

Kit and Swifty were on the road in Swifty's big Ford pickup towing Big Dave's horse trailer by 6:30 A.M. the next morning. They stopped in Pinedale to have coffee and to water the horses. After turning off highway 191 at the little crossroads of Boulder, Wyoming, they followed state road 353 to the southeast.

About seven miles into their drive, Kit yelled to Swifty to stop the truck. To their left on the north side of the road was a gated enclosure. The walls were high wire with razor wire at the top. Inside the open wire were several small buildings. The entire thing looked like some small fort. At the front was a sign that announced the facility as the property of the United States Air Force and the purpose as a research facility. They could see no vehicles nor could they see any sign of human activity.

"What the hell is that," asked Swifty?

"How the hell would I know," replied Kit.

They remained stopped in front of the facility for about five minutes but no one came forward to challenge them and there was absolutely no sign of life.

"Maybe nobody is home," said Swifty.

"Or maybe the research didn't work out and everybody in there is dead," responded Kit.

"Maybe it's a home for zombies," offered Swifty.

Kit laughed.

Swifty joined in and put the truck in gear and headed back on down the road. They drove for about twelve miles until they came to Big Sandy. Big Sandy was just a cluster of a few buildings, some of them abandoned and in various states of disrepair.

There they came to a fork in the road where a sign proclaimed that the paved road had ended.

"A real useful sign," said Swifty. "Kind of like the one at the fast food place that warns you that the coffee is hot."

They continued on the same direction, and they took the left fork to take them to Buckskin Crossing. The road went from well pressed gravel to not so smooth gravel.

"Are you sure you know where we're going?" asked Swifty.

"We're headed to the Buckskin Crossing Mercantile and Bar to see the owner, a guy named Frosty Stubbs. He bought the airplane distributor from a guy who found it in the mountains."

"And what business do we have with this Mr. Stubbs?"

"We need to find out who he bought the distributor from so we can talk to him and find out just where in the Wind River Mountains he found it."

"Supposing Mr. Stubbs doesn't want to tell us the name of the guy he bought the distributor from. What do we do then?"

"I am assuming that they may want to keep the site a secret so they can salvage surviving parts of the wreck so they can sell them. I need to convince Stubbs and the other guy that all I am interested in is recovering the remains of the pilot so he can be returned to his family. I'm hoping they will understand that and help us."

"Sounds like a lot of hope to me."

"You may be right, but it can't hurt to try."

The road was getting rougher and less like a road and more like a trail. The sagebrush was getting thicker and now was interspersed with scrub oak. The gravel road was getting harder to stay on as the terrain was getting hillier and what there was of the road on the steeper ups and downs had larger and nastier ruts.

They stopped at the top of a rise and got out to take a leak and stretch their legs. Kit took out a pair of binoculars and scanned the Wind River Mountains to their left. The mountains rose above them as a high dark mass that seemed to absorb what sunlight there was.

The cloud cover had thinned out and seemed to be breaking up with the wind. What sun did get through felt good, but Kit knew the warmth would leave as soon as the sun went down.

Old timers would tell you that spring in Wyoming lasted about two days, but it was tough to figure out when it started and when it stopped.

It was late afternoon when they were approaching the top of a rise. They could see black clouds of billowing smoke ahead of them.

"That can't be good," said Swifty.

It took them another ten minutes to get to the top of the rise and then they could see down into a small valley in front of them. At the bottom of the valley he could see a fairly wide, but shallow river running from their left to their right. The road they were on crossed over the river on a pretty substantial concrete bridge. On both sides of the bridge were trees and green grass that lined the river. The road across the bridge seemed to be coming down from higher ground and to their right a high stone wall seemed to separate the river from the hill.

About forty yards from the river was a large wooden building engulfed in flames and smoke. They could make out a small camper trailer parked some distance behind the building. In front were two old pickups and about half a block away between the road and the burning building was a white and black Ford Explorer with the markings of the Sublette County Sheriff's office. Standing next to the Explorer was what looked to be a deputy in a tan uniform wearing a dark cowboy hat.

It took almost fifteen bumpy minutes for them to drive to the bottom of the valley and park next to the Explorer.

The deputy walked over to their truck and identified himself as Deputy John Slater. Kit and Swifty introduced themselves and told Slater they were from Kemmerer.

"What happened here?" asked Kit.

"I'm not sure," said Slater. Someone at the Wine Glass Ranch must have seen the smoke and called it in to the Sheriff's office, and I was the nearest unit. I got here about thirty minutes ago and the building was engulfed in flames."

"Can we help you?" asked Kit.

"Well, if we can move those pickups we might prevent them from blowing up before the fire gets to their gas tanks."

"You got it," said Kit.

Kit and Swifty got the two pickups opened up and out of gear and after unhitching the horse trailer from Swifty's big Ford pickup, they used the truck to tow the two pickups to a safe distance.

"Can you boys keep an eye on things?" said Slater. "I need to check out the pickups and the camper out behind the main building."

Slater was gone for about fifteen minutes and then he returned to Swifty's truck. He had stopped at the Explorer and opened a cooler to extract three bottles of cold water. He shared the water with Kit and Swifty.

As Slater paused his drinking, Kit said, "Did you find anything?"

"Not much. The trucks belong to the owner, Frosty Stubbs and his bartender, a guy named Skinny. The camper out back belongs to Skinny and that's where he lives."

"Any idea where Stubbs and this Skinny guy are?"

"If Stubbs and Skinny aren't here and the trucks are, that means they could be in the building. There is no way I can find that out until this fire burns itself out and cools down."

"Do you have any help coming?"

"Yep, help is on the way, but it won't do much good till we can probe in the ruins."

"You mind if we stick around until your help arrives?" said Kit

"Actually I'd appreciate the company."

"What kind of place was this Buckskin Mercantile?"

Slater laughed. "It wasn't much, but if you were a cowboy at one of the ranches around here, it was a small oasis to drink and get a little crazy."

"Did you have trouble with drunks here?" asked Kit.

"Not really. Stubbs had a couple of cots in the back so the really drunk ones could sleep it off. He and the cowboys pretty much policed themselves. They didn't really bother anyone and we never had much trouble out here. Cowboys could go on to Pinedale, but it was real easy to get in trouble there so this was better for them and cheaper and closer to their ranches as well."

"What ranches are fairly close to here?" asked Kit.

"There are only about three ranches in this area. We're real close to the edge of the wilderness area that surrounds the mountains and that limits the land for ranches. The ranches are made up of private land and leased federal land. Course the ranches often have cattle grazing on wilderness land. Cattle ain't real good with boundaries." Slater smiled as he said that.

"Which ranch is the closest to here?" asked Kit

"The Wine Glass Ranch is about twelve miles northwest from here. The double D is about twenty-five miles south east. The Lost Creek Ranch is close to fifty miles away."

Kit thanked the deputy and walked over to Swifty's truck. He reached in the cab and came out with his map of Sublette County. He spread the map out on the hood of the truck and began to study it intensely.

"Does it show any bars nearby on that there map?" asked Swifty.

Kit looked up from the map and just rolled his eyes at Swifty.

"I'm looking to see how close these ranches are and what roads we might take to get there."

"How is that going to help us?"

"I think it's a good bet that this Stubbs guy and his bartender are toast, if you will pardon the pun."

Swifty made a face at what he considered a very bad joke.

"If Stubbs is dead, that shuts down the source of information."

"And?"

"That cowboy found the artifact while herding cattle. I think that means he worked on a nearby ranch, and he brought the artifact to Buckskin Crossing because it was reasonably close to the ranch where he worked."

"So we go to these ranches and do what?"

"We make inquiries about a cowboy finding an artifact and selling to Mr. Stubbs."

"I see something you have overlooked, genius."

"What have I overlooked?"

"I get the feeling that the Buckskin Crossing Mercantile building didn't burn down by accident. I'm guessing when the fire cools down, we'll find two bodies in there and my bet is they were dead long before the fire got to them."

"And how did you come up with that theory?"

"I don't believe in coincidence. Stubbs bought the artifact. He sold it on eBay. The sale attracted the attention of others including the two ladies back in Kemmerer. Now Stubbs is dead and his place was burned down to cover up the crime."

Kit looked at his friend and frowned. "We don't know that Stubbs is dead."

"I bet we will in about an hour."

*   *   *

Jasper Collins was wiping his horse down after a hard ride had the small mare lathered up in sweat.

Curly Polk was sitting on a small wooden stool in the adjoining tack room replacing some leather ties on his saddle.

"Looks to me like you rode that little pony pretty hard, Jasper," said Curly.

"I had no choice. I was down on the south end of the ranch when I seen this black cloud of smoke. I rode up to the top of a ridge and used my binoculars and saw the whole thing."

"What thing?"

"The Buckskin Crossing Mercantile was on fire and burning like a roman candle."

"The Buckskin Crossing Mercantile?"

"The one and only. I hightailed it back to the ranch and had it called in to the Sheriff's office. I don't know that did much good. That place was a goner."

"Did you see any sign of Stubbs or Skinny?"

"I could see their trucks parked in front and Skinny's trailer out back, but I didn't see no sign of them."

Curly emerged from the stable carrying his now repaired saddle. He was on his way to the bunkhouse when he saw Luke Code headed that way from the main house. He could see a trail of dust from the main road still hanging in the air and what looked like a black truck out in front creating the dust storm.

"Hey Luke, what's goin' on?"

"Same old, same old, Curly."

"Who was that in the black truck that just left?"

"Two ugly dudes with bad attitudes and lots of questions."

"What kind of questions?"

"It seems they're looking for Lew Cavanaugh. They claim they have some business with him and want to talk to him.

"What did you tell them?"

"I told them Lew was fence riding and wouldn't be back for two days. They said they'd be back."

"What did they look like?"

"Two hard cases. City boys from the look of them. Not nice folks."

"That's strange they'd be looking for Lew."

"I can't imagine how Lew would know two guys like that. Most of these city people have watched too much television and wind up acting weird and coming off as stupid, not tough."

"You got that right, Luke."

With that both men reached the bunkhouse and went their separate ways.

Curly sat down on his bunk and took a piece of beef jerky out of his shirt pocket and proceeded to chew on it.

He could feel his hair on his neck standing up, and he had a bad feeling in the pit of his stomach. The Buckskin Crossing Mercantile getting burned to the ground and no sign of Frosty or Skinny. Then two hard case dudes show up at the ranch looking for Lew Cavanaugh. Curly was pretty sure he was the only one who knew that Lew had found some part of an old airplane that he sold to Frosty.

If they tried to get the name from Frosty, it sounded like they managed to get Lew's name. Since Lew was due back in two days, he was pretty sure they would wait and get him when he got back to the ranch.

Why would they do any of this stuff, especially burning the mercantile. Even if there were more parts of the old airplane to salvage, they could not be worth more than a few thousand dollars. There had to be something more to this, but whatever it was, none of it was good for Lew. Maybe it was time to slip out to the north fence line and intercept Lew and let him know what was waiting for him back at the Wine Glass Ranch.

Curly grabbed his saddle bags and began to stuff Lew's few possessions into them. He would wait until dark and then head out.

CHAPTER
TEN

Help had arrived at the fire scene in Buckskin Crossing, the sheriff and two more of his deputies had showed up along with a rural fire truck and five volunteer firefighters.

The firemen used a tanker truck for a water source and added foam and were able to put the fire out pretty quickly. Not much of the mercantile building remained. A few blackened spars and parts of the framing still stood, but the rest was a smoldering soup of water, foam, ashes, and debris.

The firemen had begun searching the ashes for the cause of the fire when one of them raised his hand up and yelled for the sheriff.

Sheriff Wylie Hunt was short and lean and missing most of the hair on his head. He was about seventy years old and had been sheriff of Sublette County for almost twenty years. He was originally from North Carolina and although he had lived in Wyoming for almost thirty years, he still had a strong southern accent. When he spoke you almost expected him to say something like, "You in a heap of trouble, boy."

Sheriff Hunt made his way over to the gesturing fireman and looked down at what had been a live human being a few hours earlier.

"Any idea of who it is?" asked the sheriff.

"I think it's the owner Frosty Stubbs, although he is pretty badly burned."

"Sheriff," yelled another fireman. "We got another body over here."

As the sheriff and the firemen crowded around the second body, one of the firemen exclaimed, "Jesus Christ there's a bullet hole in the forehead."

"Oh shit", said the sheriff. "Now this damn mess is a crime scene." He motioned to his deputies to come over. "This here is a crime scene, and I want it taped off. We'll leave one deputy here to guard the scene. That'll be you, Eckert," he said to the deputy with the least seniority.

He walked to his cruiser to get on the radio so he could get his tech people out to the site as quickly as possible.

One thing the sheriff knew for sure. This was going to be an ungodly amount of paperwork.

Swifty had broken out a small propane stove and made a large pot of coffee, which he was sharing with the deputies and the volunteer firemen.

Kit accompanied deputy Slater onto the crime scene for a look at the body of Frosty Stubbs, a man he had never met. As Kit and the deputy stood over the body and studied it, Kit noticed a badly burned hammer and a pair of pliers next to the body.

"What's with the tools next to the body?" asked Kit.

"I don't know," said Slater as he bent down for a closer look.

"I think I might have an answer. Look at his toes on his right foot. Two of the bones are smashed and torn away from the foot."

"You don't suppose Stubbs was tortured by having his toes smashed with the hammer and torn off with the pliers, do you?"

The deputy stood and looked straight at Kit. "Whoever did this is one sick son-of-a-bitch."

Slater took out a small digital camera and began taking pictures.

Kit stepped out of the crime scene area as two of the deputies began to enclose the area with the familiar yellow crime scene tape.

About an hour later the sheriff, his deputies, and the volunteer firemen were gone. Deputy Eckert was standing guard over the scene as the tech squad was on its way and was still over an hour out.

Kit and Swifty had repacked their gear and were in the front seat of Swifty's Ford, drinking the last of the coffee.

"Well, do we call it quits, or do we push on.?"

"We push on," said Kit.

"The plot is getting thicker and more interesting. Who killed Stubbs and Skinny, and why? Why did they torture Stubbs and just shoot Skinny? What could the possible motive be?"

"Slater told me there was still smoldering money in the cash register, so robbery doesn't seem to fit the bill. It has to have something to do with the old airplane crash site in the Wind River Mountains. Somehow these killings are tied to that old airplane up in a snow field somewhere."

"So what do we do next?"

"We head out to the Wine Glass Ranch. That's the nearest outfit around, and we ask some questions to see if we can find out who might have sold things to Stubbs."

"Sounds like a good start to me," said Swifty. "But I think we need to be extra careful. Having two killers running around who might be interested in the same crash site we're looking for could be a problem."

"O.K. with me," said Kit as he reached for the Sublette County map and began looking for roads that would take them to the Wine Glass Ranch.

A little over an hour later, they pulled into the entrance of the Wine Glass Ranch. Both Kit and Swifty noticed the excellent condition of the buildings, barns, corrals, and fencing. Someone had set and kept a high standard for this ranch.

Swifty parked the truck in front of what looked like the bunkhouse, and he and Kit got out and stretched their legs. Their leg muscles were stiff from the constant blows the truck had taken from the bumpy road they had traveled.

Within a few minutes, a tall lanky cowboy came out of one of the barns and ambled over to where Kit and Swifty were standing.

"Kin I help you fellers?"

"You sure can. I'm Kit Andrews and this is my friend, Swifty Olson. We're from Kemmerer."

"I'm Rusty Dawkins. Glad to meet ya."

"Is your foreman around?"

"Luke? Yeah I'm pretty sure he's over to the bunkhouse," said Rusty as he pointed to a weathered one story building to their left.

"Thanks, Rusty," said Kit.

"No problem. You boys have a good day."

When they were about fifteen feet from the bunkhouse the door swung open and a short stumpy bald cowboy stepped out.

The cowboy was carrying saddlebags stuffed full, and he seemed preoccupied and almost ran into Swifty.

"Oops. I'm sorry, I didn't see you there. Can I help you with something?"

"We're looking for the foreman. A guy named Luke"?

"Luke's inside. Just go right in."

"Thanks."

"No problem."

Kit and Swifty entered the bunkhouse which was sparse and relatively clean. Kit could see about half a dozen bunks on one side of the room. A wood burning iron stove commanded the middle of the room. A couple of square tables with an assortment of chairs made up the other side of the room.

A dark haired man sat at one of the tables with a sort of account book, papers, and pencils spread out in front of him. He turned as he heard Kit and Swifty enter the bunkhouse.

"Howdy," he said as he rose to his feet. He was of medium height and his skin was burned brown from the sun. He had light blue eyes and you could almost tell from the way that he moved he was a skilled athlete.

"I'm Luke Code, foreman of the Wine Glass Ranch. What can I do for you."

Kit introduced himself and Swifty.

"You're from Kemmerer? You wouldn't be the foreman for Big Dave Carlson, would you?"

"Yes, Mr. Code, that I am."

"It's Luke. Mr. Code is my dad, and he ain't here. I know Big Dave Carlson, and I've heard about you. I read in the papers that you had some run-in with some hard cases from out of state. Was that true?"

"We did have a little trouble, but it got solved."

"Knowing Big Dave I'm sure it did. What brings you to my part of Wyoming?"

"We're doing a favor for a family back East."

"Back East?"

Kit proceeded to tell Luke about Wild Bill Hopper and his ill-fated flight in 1928. He included his encounter with the two women who were Hopper's descendants.

"I'm trying to find the cowboy who found the artifact from the crash site, so I can get a location to start searching for Hopper's remains. I figure that anyone tough enough to do what he did deserves to be found and sent home to his family."

"Well, I sure can't argue with that thinking. Do you need any help?"

"I don't think so, but I will keep that offer in mind."

"What brought you to the Wine Glass Ranch?"

"I figured that the cowboy who sold the artifact to Frosty Stubbs at Buckskin Crossing must live and work pretty close by. This is the closest ranch and there are only three in this area."

"I see what you mean. The other two ranches are northwest of here. We are spread out along the south-east edge of the Wind River Mountains The wilderness boundary makes our ranch longer and more narrow than most ranches. Do you have any idea of where the crash site might be?"

"About the only thing we know is that the crash site is supposedly in a snow field in the Wind River Mountains. Since the plane was flying from Rock Springs to Salt Lake City we are pretty sure it is on the south side of the Wind River Mountains, but we can't be sure of even that."

"Man, that's a lot of territory to cover with only two men. It would be like looking for a needle in a very large and very rugged hay stack."

"Luke, do you have any idea if any of your men might have been the one who found this artifact and sold it to Stubbs?"

Luke paused and stared at the table for a minute. "Not really. At least I haven't heard anything about it and cowboys have a hard time keeping a secret."

"Has anything unusual happened on the ranch lately or have any of your men been acting strangely."

"Hell most of my boys are pretty strange" laughed Luke.

Suddenly Luke stopped laughing and his face took on a very serious look. "There is one thing. Today two real hard cases from out of state stopped here at the ranch. They were looking for one of my men. He wasn't here. He's riding fence lines and won't be back for two days. They weren't happy about that, but they left."

"How do you know they were out of state?"

"They were hard case looking and they were wearing upscale outdoor outfits that were still stiff and new. Oh, yeah. They were wearing these brand new fancy tennis shoes in real bright colors. Not what you wear outdoors in Wyoming."

"They sure don't sound like locals."

"I heard from one of my men that the Buckskin Crossing Mercantile burned down. Did you boys happen to drive by it?"

"We got there right after one of the deputies, a guy named Slater."

"I know Slater. He usually patrols this area. He's a good hand"

"We stayed to offer what help we could. The sheriff and the fire department got there, but the building was already gone."

"What happened to Stubbs and Skinny?"

"They found them in the ashes. Both of them had been killed."

"Killed! You mean murdered in their own business! My God. What's this country coming to. I've known Stubbs for years. He was an ornery rascal, but he was fair and he was honest. He sure didn't deserve to go out that way."

"No one deserves what happened to Stubbs and his bartender."

"Was it a robbery?"

"Money was still in the cash register."

"Then why in the hell did they get killed?"

"I have no idea. My guess is that whatever went on, Stubbs and Skinny saw the faces of the killers and both were killed because they could identify the killers."

"Now I'm starting to feel all twitchy about those two hard cases I talked to today. Seems like a real odd coincidence that they show up here looking for Lew on the same day Frosty and Skinny get killed and the Mercantile gets burned down."

"You mentioned Lew. Is he the cowboy these two hard cases were looking for?"

"Yup, they were looking for Lew Cavanaugh. He's one of my hands. He's been with me for years. Lew's real quiet and stays out of trouble. He's a good worker and gets along real well with the other men. He don't mind working alone and so he's the one I usually send on the longer, lonely jobs like riding fence."

"Is Lew closer to any one of your men than the other hands. Does he have a close friend here?"

'I'd have to say that description would fit Curly Polk. They bunk next to each other and often work as a team. Polk's been here several years and he's a good hand."

"Why do they call him Curly?"

"They call him Curly because he's as bald as a bowling ball," laughed Luke.

"Is Curly around?" asked Kit.

"I saw him just before you two walked in. You might have seen him coming out of the bunkhouse."

Kit remembered the short stocky cowboy he had seen. The one who seemed preoccupied and almost ran into Swifty.

"I think we did see him."

"You boys take a load off and wait here. I'll go find him and bring him back."

"We don't want you to go to any trouble, Luke. We can find him if you tell us where to look."

"It ain't no trouble. I needed a good excuse to take a break from all this damn paperwork. It's the part of my job I like the least and I always seem to be putting it off until it's become a huge chore."

Luke pushed back his chair and stood up. He slapped his cowboy hat on his head and slipped out the door of the bunkhouse.

"So you think this Lew guy is our guy?" asked Swifty.

"My guess is that Stubbs broke under torture, gave them Lew's name and the ranch he worked at. Then they killed him and set fire to the mercantile."

"Pretty cold."

"These boys are professional killers, and cold is nothing new to them."

"What's the plan?"

"We wait to see what this Curly guy has to tell. If he is Lew's best friend, chances are he knows about the crash site or at least he knows something about the crash site. I'll bet anything that Lew showed Curly the artifact."

"Why?"

"He couldn't help himself. He probably wasn't sure of what it was and showed it to Curly to see if he might know."

"Do you think Curly did know?"

"I doubt it, but it doesn't matter. What matters is if Lew told him where he found it. Curly and Lew have been working on this ranch for years according to Luke. That tells me they know the lay of the land pretty well and would have a pretty good idea of how to find the crash site."

The bunkhouse door swung open and in walked Luke Code and Curly Polk. Luke looked upset and he had a saddlebag over his shoulder. Curly had a red face and a sheepish look like a kid caught with his hand in the cookie jar.

"I just found Curly in the stable with his saddlebag stuffed full with Lew's stuff."

"I wasn't stealing it. Lew's my best friend. I was gonna take it to him."

"Take it to him where?" asked Kit.

"I know the route he follows when he's riding fence line and I planned to slip out tonight and intercept him and give him his stuff."

"Why would you intercept him?"

"Cause I know those two city dudes were here today looking for him, and he don't know no city dudes."

"That hardly seems like a good reason to clean out his stuff and take it out to him on the fence line, Curly."

Curly did not answer and stood looking intently at the floor.

"Why don't you have a seat, Curly, and we can talk this over."

Curly slowly looked up and then looked at Kit, Luke, and Swifty. He stepped forward and pulled out a chair at the table and sat down.

Swifty, Kit, and Luke joined him at the table. Kit waited a minute and then started talking to Curly.

"Is there a reason Lew should be afraid of those two city slickers? Is there some reason you might be afraid of them?"

"I ain't afraid of no city slickers," said Curly.

"If you aren't afraid of them, then why all the drama? What aren't you telling us, Curly? We're here to get Lew's help. We have no reason to hurt him or you."

Curly looked at Kit, paused, and then began to speak. "I heard that old man Stubbs and Skinny got killed and then the mercantile was set on fire with them in it. Right after that those two city boys showed up looking for Lew. I figured that they went to Stubbs to find out who sold him that old airplane part and when he wouldn't tell them, they beat him until he did and then they killed him. I figure they got Lew's name from Stubbs and now they are after him."

Curly paused as if to take a breath and then began again. "Lew is my best friend. I don't want to see him hurt or killed. I want to help him get the hell out of here where those two assholes can't find him."

"I don't blame you for trying to help Lew. I'd do the same thing if he was my friend," said Kit.

"Maybe it would help if we told you why we are trying to find Lew. We want his help and have no reason to hurt him," added Swifty.

"What kind of help do you want from Lew?"

Kit leaned back in his chair and began to tell Curly the story of Wild Bill Hopper and his air mail flight in 1928. When he was finished he could tell he had Curly's rapt attention.

"Mr. Andrews, that sounds like some sort of movie thing, not like real life."

'I assure you, Curly, it is a true story and Swifty and I are trying to find the crash site so we can try to locate Mr. Hopper's remains and get them shipped back to his family for closure and a proper burial."

"Then what are those two city assholes looking for that they don't mind killing and burning people up?"

"I have no idea, Curly. I think it is somehow connected to the plane crash site, but what it is I don't know."

"We no longer believe in coincidences," said Swifty.

"I don't think all these things are a coincidence either," said Kit.

"Well what are we gonna do?" asked Curly.

"We need to talk to Lew and find out how to get to the crash site."

"You're welcome to stay with us and wait for Lew to arrive. It's only two days," said Luke.

"That's very generous, Luke, but if we wait for Lew to get here, it will get a little crowded with the two hard cases likely to come back and they might come back with some of their friends."

"You're right, Kit, I forgot about that."

"Maybe Swifty and I could ride with Curly and intercept Lew on the fence line. We could talk with him and not get near the main ranch."

Curly was quiet and did not immediately respond to Kit's idea.

"What do you think, Curly?" asked Kit.

Curly looked up at Kit. "So all you want from Lew is where he found that old airplane part?"

"That's right, Curly, that's all we want to talk to him about."

"Well maybe there's no need for you to make that ride to the fence line with me."

"What do you mean, Curly?"

"Lew and me were just finished rounding up the spring cattle strays and had them corralled in a box canyon. That night he showed me this strange looking metal cylinder thing. He told me he found it in a snow field when he was pulling out a calf that got stuck in the soft snow. He asked me what it was, and I had no idea. He found some markings on it and said he thought it was from some kind of airplane. I kidded him that it was probably from a space ship."

"When I asked him where he found it, he kind of clammed up and said he never said anything about where he found it. I didn't say anything else and after a while I guess he felt kind of guilty or foolish and he told me where he found it."

Silence filled the room. Finally Kit broke the silence by pulling his chair up to the table and leaning forward towards Curly.

"Can you tell us where the crash site is, Curly?"

"I'll try, but you might want to write this down as it ain't so easy to remember if you ain't familiar with the country."

Luke got up and went over to the other table where his journal and papers were scattered and returned with a blank sheet of paper and a pencil. He handed the paper and pencil to Kit.

"Lew said he found the lost cattle after tracking them into the wilderness area of the Wind River Mountains. They were grazing near the edge of a snow field. The snow field was several feet higher than the meadow and there was lots of water running in small streams, runoff from the snow melt."

"The cattle held when he slowly rode up and then one calf took off up the bank and onto the snow field. Lew gave chase on his horse and after a short run, the calf slipped in the soft snow and got stuck. Lew dismounted to pull the calf out and when he pulled the calf free, it took off bawling for his mama. Lew looked down where he had pulled the calf from the snow and there was a black metal cylinder with some markings on it. Lew pulled it free from the snow and stuck it in his saddlebags and then he herded the cattle back to the box canyon corral we had set up."

"Lew described the place as the south end of a long fairly narrow snow field elevated up several feet from the meadow. This snow field was just north of the head of the lower fork of Squaw Creek. There are five fingers running off Squaw Creek near its head."

"Lew said it was the finger that runs mostly to the north that he followed to the snow field. He said that you was to stand where he stood and looked up, you'd be looking at the south edge of Knife's Edge glacier. Knife's Edge is the high narrow glacier at the very top of the south end of the Wind River Mountains. That glacier is very narrow at the top and the sides of the mountain there are very steep. The glacier runs straight down both sides like a saddle on a skinny horse."

Curly stopped talking and took in a deep breath like he was starving for oxygen.

Kit looked at the notes he had written down on paper and he proceeded to copy the notes into the note section of his iPhone.

When he was done, Kit said, "Luke, I think we need to make a plan."

"What plan you got in mind, Kit?"

"You let Curly go out and intercept Lew and let him know what's going on and about the two ass holes who might be waiting here for him in two days. Let Lew decide what he wants to do. If he wants to disappear for a while, he needs to make it to Kemmerer and see Woody Harrison. He's my attorney and a good friend of Big Dave."

"That sounds like a seal of approval to me," said Luke.

"I'll call Woody by satellite phone and he can provide Lew with a place to stay and some money. Nobody in Kemmerer will know Lew is hiding out there except for Woody and Big Dave."

Kit took a piece of blank paper from the table and scribbled out a note addressed to Lew Cavanaugh. Then he handed the note to Curly.

"This tells Woody and Big Dave who Lew is and what I need them to do for him. Give it to Lew when you see him."

"What about the two hard cases? They'll be coming back," said Luke.

"Just tell them that Lew still hasn't showed up and you aren't sure when he might come in, Luke. That should get them out of your hair."

"And what are you and Swifty going to do?"

"We're going airplane hunting" said Swifty with a smile.

*   *   *

CHAPTER
ELEVEN

Within half an hour Curly had departed on horseback with a cloth bag tied to his saddle horn containing all of Lew's possessions from the bunkhouse.

Kit and Swifty had a topographical map spread out on one of the tables in the bunkhouse and were going over it with Luke who had a better working knowledge of the area than they did.

"Looks to me like you need to drive to this point here on the map; that is just short of the boundary for the wilderness area. Where you want to go is slightly northeast of there. You need to pick up Squaw Creek and then slowly work your way north to northwest."

"Why don't we just use the GPS to mark the longitude and latitude on this map for the site of Squaw Creek?" asked Kit.

"Every year runoff from the mountains changes and so does the location of the creek. That's why you got to be sure you are on Squaw Creek. When you get up there you will see more streams and more water than you've ever seen in Wyoming. The spring runoff creates all these streams and then in the fall they just disappear."

Kit and Swifty shook hands with Luke and climbed into Swifty's Ford truck. They waved good-bye as they turned the truck and drove out back to entrance to the Wine Glass Ranch.

They drove slowly on the bumpy and rutted road. After a few minutes Swifty stopped the truck and turned off the ignition. He turned to Kit with a hard look in his eyes.

"This ain't going to be no picnic, Kit. We got to treat this like a combat mission. We don't know who all we are up against, but we do know some of them are armed and very dangerous. At least one group of these boys ain't the least bit reluctant to kill anyone that gets in their way, and they don't give a rat's ass about the law."

"Why do you say groups?"

"Think about it. We got one group of two hard cases who are killers. We got another group of two ladies who sure as hell ain't telling us the truth. God knows if there are any more."

"Why would there be groups. What could they possibly be after in a one hundred year old crash site of a mail plane?"

"That's what's bothering me. They sure as hell ain't interested in no old plane wreck. I doubt there was anything in some letters worth killing for after almost a hundred years. I think we missed something and it was probably right in front of us and we missed it."

"What would there be we could have missed? We got an old plane, a dead pilot, and a bag of U.S. mail."

"Maybe there was something else in that mail pouch. Maybe they didn't just haul mail back in them days."

"I can't imagine that they could have been hauling anything of size or weight. It wouldn't have been possible in that old plane."

"When you was looking into this old Wild Bill Hopper fella, did you Google him?"

"Google him? I didn't think you even knew what that meant. Now that I think of it, I used the internet for maps and data about the area, but I didn't Google Hopper."

"Maybe we should."

"How we gonna do that? There's no network out here. There isn't any cell phone service either."

"Just before we get to the wilderness area there's a ranger station on that map. If it's manned, I bet they got a satellite connection available that we could borrow."

"You know, for a beat up old cowpoke, that's a pretty good idea."

Swifty grinned at Kit, turned in his seat and started the truck. He put the truck in gear and they proceeded on their slow, bumpy ride.

After about an hour's drive they came to a junction in the road. According to the GPS they had been driving east on Emigrant Road and a sign by the side of the road said if they continued on Emigrant Road it would be 28 miles to Highway 28. If they took the left fork, they would be on Forest Service Road 850. They turned left on Forest Service Road 850 and continued on a northerly route. After a couple of roads exited to the east, they came to a junction. The left fork took them to Bear Trap and staying on #850 would take them to Dutch Joe Guard Station, which was their destination.

Twenty minutes later they pulled into what resembled a parking area by the Dutch Joe Guard Station. The station was a Forest Service cabin and was named after Dutch Joe Creek. The creek was located just northwest of the cabin by about a quarter of a mile.

The flagpole in front of the cabin sported a fairly new American flag, and an old Forest Service pickup truck painted a fading light green was parked in front of the cabin.

Kit and Swifty went into the cabin and were greeted by a ranger in his twenties.

"Good evening, gentlemen. I was just getting ready to close up. I'm Stephen Nix, but everyone calls me Nix." The young ranger was average height and had a slight build. His brown hair was closely cropped unlike many of the younger Rangers Kit had encountered who wore their hair in a stylishly long fashion. Kit noted that his uniform was clean and only slightly wrinkled.

Kit introduced himself and Swifty and told the Ranger they planned to camp by the cabin for the night and asked if it were all right to unload and hobble their horses by the cabin.

"Of course. Please be my guest. Feel free to use the well in the back for you and your horses. Do you need anything else from me?"

"Thank you, Ranger Nix. We appreciate your hospitality. We'd be pleased if you joined us for breakfast in the morning."

"I'd be pleased to join you. It's pretty early in the season, and I haven't seen many people out here this month."

Kit and Swifty shook hands good-bye and went out to the truck and trailer. They unloaded the horses and while Kit set up feed bags with oats for the three horses, Swifty took three buckets and filled them with water from the pump. By the time he got back, Kit had hobbled the horses and Swifty set a bucket down in front of each animal.

With the horses cared for they set up camp around a raised metal grill and pulled out sleeping bags and cooking gear and food. It didn't take long for Kit to build a fire and Swifty took two small, but thick steaks out of the cooler and after rubbing salt and pepper into the steaks he put them on the now hot grill. While he was monitoring the steaks, Kit made a salad out of greens, onions, radishes, and tomatoes and tossed it in a large old wooden bowl.

In less than twenty minutes they sat down on a nearby picnic table to a tasty steak dinner accompanied by several cans of very cold beer.

Kit had placed a Coleman lantern on the table as the sun had gone down, and the light had disappeared.

They finished their meal and cleaned up by lantern light and slipped into their sleeping bags using their saddles for pillows.

"How cold do you think it gets here this time of year?" asked Swifty.

"We could easily have frost on top of us by morning."

"It's late May and everyone, including the weather is confused except me," retorted Swifty.

There was no reply from Kit. He was already fast asleep.

CHAPTER TWELVE

Kit and Swifty were up at dawn. Kit fed and watered the horses and Swifty started the fire and began to prepare breakfast. Kit rolled up their sleeping bags and stored them in the truck.

Just as Swifty was spooning scrambled eggs out of the skillet, young Ranger Nix made his appearance.

"Wow, you guys are early birds. I can't believe you have breakfast ready this early."

"Have a seat young Mr. Nix, I am about to surprise and delight your taste buds," said Swifty.

"Thank you, Mr. Swifty."

The three of them sat down on the picnic table and ate scrambled eggs, sausage and fried potatoes and hot coffee. Swifty poured catsup on his eggs and a watchful young Nix did likewise.

After they had finished their breakfast and were drinking a second cup of coffee, Kit began explaining why they were stopped at the Dutch Joe Creek Guard Station.

"We're looking for an airplane crash site in the wilderness area of the Wind River Mountains."

"An airplane crash! I've been here two months, and I never heard anything about any airplane crash up here?"

"This particular airplane crash took place in 1928."

"1928! And you're just looking now?"

Kit explained the story of Bill Hooper, the crash, the discovery of the artifact, and the search by his relatives to find his remains and take them back to South Carolina.

"That is quite a story, Mr. Andrews."

"You can call me Kit. Everyone else does."

Nix smiled and looked at Swifty. "Is Swifty your real name?"

Swifty grinned and said, "I could tell you my real name, but then I'd have to shoot you."

Nix paused and then began to laugh, as he realized that Swifty was kidding him.

"So, do you have any idea where this crash site might be? The Wind River Mountain Range is a huge area. The Wind River Range totals 2.25 million acres and runs 110 miles from Togwotee Pass in the north to South Pass in the south. The range averages 35 to 40 miles wide. There are over 48 mountain peaks higher than 12,500 feet. Every afternoon brings thunderstorms and lightning and we've got black bears, grizzly bears, mountain lions, and wolves."

Nix paused, as though to catch his breath. "Plus you are headed for a wilderness area so no motorized vehicles allowed, but I guess that's why you brought horses."

"You guessed right, Nix. Walking is downright offensive to a cowboy."

"Do you have some sort of starting point like a landmark or something?"

"The only landmark we have is Squaw Creek."

"Well, that poses a bit of a problem."

"Why is that?"

"Squaw Creek has three branches coming out of the mountains. There's west fork which is just north of here, the middle fork and east fork, which are south of here."

"You mean there are actually three Squaw Creeks!"

"You could certainly say that."

"So how far from here going by Squaw Creek west fork is it to the Wind River Mountains?"

"I'd say it's close to ten miles, but you have to remember that you are gradually going uphill all the way."

"That is all very helpful, Nix," said Kit. "Can you tell me if you have access to the internet at this camp?"

"No, I don't. I wish I did. Internet access would make the quiet times a lot more interesting."

"How do you communicate with your boss or Ranger Headquarters?"

"I have a satellite phone I can use. I have a diesel generator so I can keep charging the batteries if I need to."

"I was hoping that I could get internet access, but I guess not."

"When I need to know something I just call on the satellite phone and have headquarters look it up for me."

Kit looked at Swifty who had a smirk on his face. "Yeah, one could certainly do that."

"Nix, is it all right with you if we leave our truck and trailer parked here while we do our exploring on horseback? If it's all right with you, we'd like to use this location as a base camp. It might be several days."

"It's fine with me. This is all public land around the station. I'll be sure to keep an eye on them, but like I said before, I haven't seen many people out here this early in the season."

"You didn't happen to see a couple of tough looking guys in a black SUV, did you?"

"No, I haven't seen anyone like that. You two are the first folks I've seen in at least three days."

Kit and Swifty turned down Nix's offer to help clean up and after about an hour they had loaded up their pack horse and were prepared to leave.

Nix came out of the cabin to see them off, and he noticed both Kit and Swifty had rifles in their saddle scabbards.

"What kind of gun is that, Mr. Andrews?"

Kit smiled and pulled the rifle out of the scabbard for Nix to look at. "This is an AR-10, chambered in .308 caliber."

"Is that little square thing on top of it a scope?"

"Actually it's a holographic scope. It shows a red dot, but doesn't magnify the view."

"It's a rugged looking weapon."

"It's meant to be, so it survives rough treatment without a problem."

"Well, that makes sense, because we got plenty of rough treatment in these mountains."

"Thanks for all of your help, Nix. We'll be back by nightfall."

"Take care Mr. Andrews. You too, Mr. Swifty."

Kit and Swifty turned their horses north toward the west branch of Squaw Creek.

*   *   *

Kit waited until they had ridden about a mile from the ranger station and had reached the top of a small rise. He brought his horse to a halt and Swifty rode his horse up next to Kit.

"What's up?"

"I'm going to see if I can raise Woody on the satellite phone."

Kit reached back into his saddle bag and pulled out the brick-like bulky satellite phone. He turned the phone on and waited for about a minute until he saw he had a connection and then he dialed the number for Woody's office.

Woody's secretary answered and promptly connected Kit with Woody.

"This must be a very expensive phone call from one of those new gadgets you are always buying."

"You are correct, Woody."

"What can I do for you today, Mr. Andrews?"

"You can do me a favor by getting me some information that I should have gotten before I started on this trip."

"What information is that?"

"I'd like you to Google that lady who claims to be William Hopper's grand-daughter and her alleged daughter as well."

"And what am I looking for?"

"I'd like to know if they really are who they say there are."

"Of course, I'll get on it right away."

"I'd also like you to Google Mr. Hopper as well as his last flight. I think there is something very odd about all this interest in some hundred year old air mail, and a little research may tell us what that is."

"I'll see what I can find out. How do I get back to you with the information?"

"Since I have a good signal here we'll stay at this location and wait for your call."

Kit then gave Woody the number for his satellite phone and ended the call.

"We might as well rest here a bit and wait for Woody's call," said Kit.

Both he and Swifty dismounted and after tying off their horses and the pack horse, they shared a canteen of water while they waited for Woody's call.

About ten minutes later Kit's satellite phone chirped, and he quickly answered it.

"Well Mr. Andrews it seems your suspicions were well founded."

"What did you find out?"

"First of all, Ms. Louise Stout is not the grand-daughter of Mr. Hopper. He never married and had no children. It appears as though his only living relatives are a couple of children of a nephew who was a son of his brother, Thomas Hopper."

"So she's a phony."

"It certainly appears so."

"Why would she and the other woman put on a scam to try to find Hopper's remains?"

"The answer to that excellent question is in the second part of my research."

"And that would be?"

"Mr. Hopper was not only carrying air mail envelopes. He was also carrying a small metal box containing ten pounds of cut and polished diamonds."

"Did you say ten pounds of diamonds?"

"Your hearing is excellent, Mr. Andrews, ten pounds of diamonds."

"Now all this crazy stuff that has been happening makes some sense."

"It certainly does."

"Thanks for all your help, Woody."

"You're welcome. Let me know if you need anything else."

"We'll be in touch," said Kit as he shut off the phone.

"Ten pounds of diamonds!" said Swifty."

"Cut and polished."

"Well there ain't no doubt that diamonds is one thing that would survive even a nasty plane crash and fire and then being buried in the snow and ice for years."

"It would appear that someone sent the two women to try to get us to find the crash site so they could find the diamonds," said Kit.

"Could be anyone who was smart enough to figure out that old airplane part came from Hopper's airplane and made the connection to the missing diamonds. Sounds like professional treasure hunters to me."

"Yeah, but aren't most of those professional treasure hunters working for legitimate companies or corporations? I mean real for-profit companies that pay taxes and all that good stuff?" asked Kit.

"Now I understand why that woman wanted me to sign the non-disclosure agreement. She needed to keep me quiet about what we really found at the crash site."

"I suppose even companies that pay taxes use tricks and do some sleazy stuff to beat out their competition," said Swifty.

"I have a hard time believing that a company would condone beatings, torture, murder, and burning down other people's property to get an edge on a competitor."

"Maybe not all treasure hunters are honest companies. Maybe we are dealing with some real pond scum level crooks," said Swifty.

"Now that I think about it, maybe we are dealing with more than one group of treasure hunters. One might be a legitimate company and one might just be a sophisticated gang of thieves."

"So how do we tell who is who? Does one group wear white hats and one group wear black hats?"

"That's very funny, Swifty. We have no idea of who is who, but one thing seems pretty clear."

"What's that?"

"If Lew Cavanagh took our advice and is hiding out at Big Dave's place, then no one else except Curly Polk and Luke Code know about the location of the crash site. Whoever these treasure dudes are, they won't know that and will be following us to see if we can find the crash site for them."

"So if we do find the crash site, I take it they don't plan to reward us?" said Swifty.'

"Finding the crash site and finding a small metal box of diamonds are two different things. If we do find the diamonds, I don't think these treasure hunters plan on letting us keep them. They just need us to do all the hard work, and then they swoop in and grab the diamonds."

"I take a dim view of vultures and if these dudes do swoop in, they might just get their asses shot off."

"We've got to find the crash site first and there are a lot of large rocks and mountains in front of us."

Swifty did not reply.

"What? No smart remark Swifty?"

Swifty looked up at Kit and grinned. "I just wish I had brought more ammunition. Hunting works both ways."

*   *   *

Kit and Swifty rode slowly on a southeasterly course until they hit Trail Creek. They rode along the banks of the creek for about four miles until they came to where the creek ran into Squaw Creek, which was about twice the size of Trail Creek, but still only about ten feet across from bank to bank.

They followed Squaw Creek in a northerly direction for almost two miles. The creek bank rose and fell with more frequency, and the landscape became much more hilly the further they went.

Kit could tell they were slowly gaining altitude as the grassy areas were less frequent and the rocky areas more pronounced.

Finally they came to where the creek seemed to split into three creeks, each of which seemed to be coming from the Wind River Mountains that seemed to stretch across the entire horizon to the north.

Kit and Swifty paused to let their horses drink from the creek.

"Which fork do we take," asked Swifty?

"Let's start with the one to the east and work our way to the west," replied Kit.

They headed up the east fork of Squaw Creek toward the mountain range to the north.

The trail that seemed to follow the banks of the creek became narrower and steeper and no longer ran just parallel to the creek bed. Instead the trail wove back and forth in between rocks of ever increasing size. Some of the rocks were so large that they completely lost sight of the creek. After about two miles of following this steep and meandering trail Kit signaled a halt to Swifty.

Both men dismounted and paused to stretch their legs. Kit took out his GPS and waited for it to acquire at least three satellites. After a few minutes the GPS had a solid connection and gave them their current position and their current altitude.

"We're at about 8,500 feet," said Kit.

"How high is this Knife's Edge glacier?" asked Swifty.

"I think the top is about 12,000 feet."

"This trail keeps getting steeper and narrower the higher we go."

"Not to mention it seems to get more twisty as well. Half of the time we can't even see the creek," said Kit.

"Well we're not making any progress standing here," said Swifty as he swung up into the saddle.

Kit smiled and also swung himself into his saddle and followed Swifty's lead. They had taken turns leading the pack horse and now it was Kit's turn.

After another hour of slow, uphill climbing Swifty motioned for a halt. He and Kit dismounted and tied off their horses to some nearby brush.

While Kit consulted his GPS, Swifty took out his binoculars and swung them to the north.

"I see some kind of rounded peak that looks to be about a mile to the north. It's kind of strange looking."

"That would be the peak called the Crow's Nest," said Kit.

"According to my map and the GPS that peak should be about as far up as this fork of Squaw Creek goes. The spring that starts this creek along with runoff from the mountains should be near that peak."

"Is the snowfield near the Crow's Nest?"

"I have no idea. The map doesn't show snow fields, just the topography of the land and the locations of the waterways, roads, and trails."

"I doubt you will find any roads up here."

"As small as this trail is getting we will probably have a hard time finding trails as well."

The two men remounted their horses and resumed their journey up the steep and narrow trail. They rode for another twenty minutes when they decided to stop and dismount.

"Looks like we walk and lead the horses for the next part of this trail," said Kit.

"God, I hate walking. Makes me think I'm back in the infantry."

"Maybe we should change footwear," said Kit.

"Good idea. This country wasn't made for hiking in cowboy boots."

Both men had packed well-worn hiking boots in bags contained on the pack horse. Within minutes they had changed footwear and each of them had also added a fleece vest to their clothing.

"It's getting cooler as we get higher."

"At least the weather still looks good," replied Swifty.

"As we get higher, afternoon thunderstorms with lightning become a real possibility. Not to mention the occasional spring snowstorm."

"It's springtime in Wyoming. I was once told that spring in Wyoming usually lasted about a day. Two if you were lucky."

"High altitude changes everything. You never know what kind of weather you might get."

Their progress slowed as they walked on the steep, narrow and twisting trail. They had to step carefully as occasionally their footsteps caused loose rocks to cascade down the trail behind them.

Finally they reached the base of Crow's Nest and as they went around the eastern side of the base of the peak, they found the spring that was the starting point of the west fork of Squaw Creek.

"This looks like a good place to break for lunch," said Kit.

"Can't happen soon enough for me. All this uphill climbing has made me tired and hungry. What's for lunch?"

"Hot dogs, beans, and rolls," replied Kit. Swifty took the horses to the spring to water them and then tied off the horses while Kit unpacked the small propane stone and his cooking gear and food box. Soon he had everything done, and they sat in the shade of a large boulder and ate their lunch.

"So we made it to the Crow's Nest and the beginning of the west fork of Squaw Creek. What do we do now?"

"We climb part way up the Crow's Nest and look for snow fields," answered Kit.

"Somehow I don't think that is going to be quite as easy as it sounds."

"You're probably right, but we won't know until we get up there and take a look around."

Both men cleared away their lunch gear and repacked it. Kit washed out their cooking and eating gear in the downside of the spring and when they were finished, they started looking for a trail that led up into the Crow's Nest.

They hadn't walked very far around the base of the peak before Swifty found a faint trail starting behind a large sagebrush.

They carefully picked their way up the narrow trail until they were about a hundred feet up from the base of the peak.

Swifty took out his binoculars and began scanning the horizon between their position and the mountain range to the north.

Swifty scanned the area in slow sweeps from left to right and adjusting his vision slightly higher after each complete sweep of the horizon.

He could see several small snowfields, but nothing like he expected to see. Most of them were either very narrow or very short. He picked out two that he thought might work and made notes on his smart phone. Swifty was putting his binoculars away when Kit touched him on the shoulder and said "What's that?"

Swifty followed Kit's arm and extended finger toward a thin plume of smoke from behind a small ridge of rocks just to the north of them.

"Only one way to find out," said Swifty and they both began to descend from the Crow's Nest on the narrow and treacherous trail.

Once they reached the base of the peak they untied their horses and led them on foot towards the source of the smoke.

CHAPTER THIRTEEN

Neither man spoke as they slowly made their way toward the low wall of rocks between them and the visible smoke plume. When they got within about two hundred yards Swifty motioned for Kit to take his horse's reins and Swifty melted into the nearby sagebrush.

Kit knew that Swifty was going to work his way around so he could flank the location of the smoke and get a good look at what was causing the plume. Kit waited patiently for Swifty's return. About fifteen minutes later Swifty reappeared as silently as he had vanished.

"What's the situation?" asked Kit.

"Some old guy is sitting around a small campfire singing to himself. He's got a mule loaded with gear tied off to a nearby tree."

"He's singing to himself?"

"He actually has a pretty good voice, for an old fart."

"Is he a potential problem?"

"If he is, then I'm a piss poor judge of character."

Kit looked questioningly at Swifty, but all Swifty did was smile back with that sort of laughing look in his eyes.

"The old dude is sitting by a campfire singing barbershop quartet songs to his mule."

"What!"

Swifty was already headed for the site of the campfire. Kit followed.

They each led their horses and as they got close to the rock wall, Swifty yelled out, "Hello the camp."

"Hello yerself, and who in the hell is wandering around in my back yard?"

As they rounded the edge of the rock wall both of them could see the source of Swifty's amusement.

A broad shouldered man of middle age or older sat on a camp stool next to a small campfire. He had brown curly hair and a goatee like beard. He was wearing a St. Louis Cardinal's baseball Jersey over a long sleeved tee shirt. He had on brown canvas pants with well-worn work boots. Plopped on his head was a black derby hat. He had a bright red bandanna tied around his neck. He wore a hunting knife in a sheath on his belt, but no other weapons were visible. A coffee pot was resting on some rocks that surrounded the small campfire.

"Well looky here. Either you boys are lost or I'm having a bad dream as a result of my questionable cooking skills."

"Howdy, mister," said Kit and Swifty touched the front of his cowboy hat.

"Since you seem to be talking at me, it can't be a bad dream so you must be lost."

Kit stepped forward and extended his right hand. "I'm Kit Andrews and this here is my friend, Swifty Olson."

All three men shook hands and Swifty commented, "You don't seem surprised to see us."

The man with the derby hat smiled and said, "I heard you coming about twenty minutes ago, and I smelled you coming almost an hour ago."

Swifty and Kit smiled at that and the man with the derby hat said, "Where are my manners? I've spent too much time out here alone. Please allow me to introduce myself. My name is O.J. Pratt. I'm a prospector in the summer and a trapper in the winter."

"I thought prospecting and trapping in a wilderness area was illegal," said Swifty.

"Oh I'm sure it is, but I try not to pay too much attention to laws and rules and such. If you live yer life by the government rules, then it can't be much of a life. You might as well just shoot yourself. I used to be an auctioneer back in the Midwest. I finally got tired of too many people around me all the time and all of them bitching and bellyaching and decided to find a new line of work that suited me better."

"How long have you been living and working up here in the Wind River Mountains, Mr. Pratt?" asked Kit.

"Call me O.J. sonny. Everyone else does. Mr. Pratt was my daddy. He was an auctioneer too. He used to practice at the dinner table by auctioning off each part of our supper. He's gone now, God rest his soul.

Now back to your question, Mr. Andrews. I've been up in these mountains for nine years, more or less."

"Nine years? Do you come down and go into a town or somewhere for supplies."

"I usually get supplies twice a year from a little place called Buckskin Crossing Mercantile. I sell my furs to the owner and spend the money on supplies. I keep the gold I find. The old guy running the place is a little crusty and tough, but he runs an honest store."

"You mean Frosty Stubbs?"

"Yes, I think Stubbs is his name. Do you know him?"

"Never met him, but he and his bartender were murdered a couple of days ago and the killers burned the mercantile to the ground."

"Murdered! Stubbs! By who?"

"We don't know, but we heard that the sheriff is looking for a couple of suspects. They were described as two tough looking dudes from the east."

"Well, it looks like I'll have to find a new place to get supplies. I liked that mercantile. It had what I needed and wasn't too dang expensive."

O.J. paused and looked carefully at Kit and Swifty and their horses.

"You boys don't look like cowboys and you don't look like tree-huggers and you sure as hell don't look like the law. Just what are you two doing up here where nobody ever comes unless they're lost?"

Kit smiled and he and Swifty tied off their horses and sat down on nearby rocks.

"We're up here looking for the site of an airplane crash."

"Airplane crash? Up here? I ain't even seen an airplane near here in nine years. You boys really are lost."

"This crash happened in 1928."

"1928! Took yer time getting up here, didn't yah?" laughed O.J.

Kit went on to tell the story of Bill Hopper and his ill-fated flight. When he was done, O.J. was staring into the coals of his dying campfire. He looked up at Kit and Swifty.

"If such a plane crashed in a snowfield and some cowboy found a part of it in the snowfield, then there ain't many places around here that would qualify as possible landing sites. I know this part of the mountains better than anyone and I've probably walked across all the snowfields near the headwaters of the Squaw Creek. I've never seen anything like the airplane part or artifact or whatever you called it."

"Where do you stay in the winter O.J.? I know it can get pretty nasty up here and snow storms can happen even in the summer."

"Over the years I've found a series of caves as I've looked for gold and silver and also when I'm out trapping for critters in the winter. I have about four caves that are big enough to hole up in for quite a spell. I've provisioned each of them so I can survive until a storm blows over. I've found some smaller caves I've used, but they aren't very big and other than firewood, I've stored nothing in them."

"I'm a little surprised to hear about caves up here. We came all the way up from Dutch Joe's, and I saw very little that looked like a cave," said Swifty.

O.J. looked at Swifty and paused for a moment, as if he was sizing Swifty up.

"The bigger caves are higher up at about 10,000 feet. I found most of the caves over by the west fork of Squaw Creek. If you boys are searching all the forks of Squaw Creek, you'll probably get to see some of them when you get to the west fork."

"Thanks for the tips," said Swifty.

"You're welcome, Swifty."

"If you live up here all the time, what do you do for entertainment?" asked Kit.

"Every day I've got a front row seat to the greatest show on earth. The animals, the rocks, the birds, the weather, it all takes part in putting on a show for me. Then, of course, on occasion I feel moved to sing."

"Sing?"

"Sing, you know make musical noise."

"Out here, by yourself?"

"It's usually in response to what I have just seen in nature. I used to sing in a barbershop quartet. We sang harmonizing music. I like singing my part and imagining that the other guys are singing along with me."

"So you don't sing rock and roll?" asked Kit.

"And you don't sing country and western?" added Swifty.

"Actually I sing anything I can get away with and still remember the verses," laughed O.J.

"Would you boys like a sample?"

"I think we'll pass on that, O.J."

"We looked at a couple of possible snow field sites from up on the Crow's Nest, O.J. I marked them on this map. Does this jive with where you were talking about as possible landing sites?"

O.J. studied the map and then turned it sideways and then back.

"Those are about the same ones I was thinking of."

"O.J. have you seen any other people up here in the past day or so?"

"No, Kit, I can't say that I have."

"Do you see many people up here in the summertime?"

"There are the usual groups of backpackers and occasionally some goofy birdwatchers, but I might go a whole summer and only see a dozen people. I usually smell them or hear them coming, and I tuck myself away in the rocks until they're gone. Like I said earlier, I've had my fill of people."

Kit reached inside his jacket and pulled out a plastic zip-lock bag. He took out a piece of jerky and offered it to O.J.

O.J. eagerly accepted the jerky and immediately began chewing on it.

"Thanks, Kit, this is one thing I miss when I run out and I haven't tasted jerky in over three months."

"Here, O.J., keep the bag," said Kit as he tossed rest of the bagged jerky over to O.J.

"Thank you kindly, Kit. This is much appreciated."

Swifty got to his feet quickly followed by Kit. "We got to head out, O.J. and start looking over those two snow fields so we can get back to camp by nightfall."

"Where are you boys camped?"

"We have our truck and supplies at Dutch Joe Station."

"Well you boys take care of yourselves, and I'll keep an eye peeled for that there plane wreck. Although I can't imagine what's left of it since 1928," laughed O.J.

The three men shook hands and Kit and Swifty led their horses as they headed uphill on a faint trail in the rocks toward the first of the two snow fields that Swifty had marked on the map.

*   *   *

The first snowfield was narrow and quite long. The snow was soft, so Swifty broke out the aluminum snow shoes from the pack horse and the two of them trudged across the length of the snow field keeping about five yards between them and began to search in a grid format and when they reached end of the field, they moved over five yards and trudged back the way they had come.

It took them almost two hours to cover the field in their crossing pattern, and they found nothing. They took a water break and then moved on to the second snowfield which was much shorter, but also much wider. They re-donned the snow shoes and began making their way across the field this time going across the width of the field, not the length. Again they found nothing. When they had finished, they packed up their gear and made their way back down along the trail they had followed up to the snowfields.

When they came to the campsite where they had seen O.J., there was no sign of him and even the small campfire had been covered over with dirt and rocks so that there was no evidence anyone had been there.

It was almost dark by the time they got back to Dutch Joe Station and after a hurried supper, they were quick to slip into their sleeping bags and soon the night air was dominated by silence.

CHAPTER FOURTEEN

Morning came too early for the tired duo. Kit rustled up breakfast while Swifty packed away their gear.

"Is that invitation for breakfast still good?" asked a smiling Nix as he walked out of the cabin with an empty coffee cup in his hand.

"Of course it is," said Kit. "Coffee pot is on the little stove. Help yourself."

Within ten minutes, the three men sat down at the picnic table to a hearty breakfast of eggs, ham, and potatoes.

In between bites of food, Nix asked the two men how their hunt for the crash site had gone.

"We saw a lot of snow and not much else," replied Kit.

"We did see a crazy old coot up above the Crow's Nest," said Swifty.

"He's a real colorful character."

"What did he look like?" asked Nix.

"He looked like any old geezer camping up in the mountains. Just him and his mule."

Kit was not interested in revealing to Nix that O.J. made his living by illegally prospecting and trapping in a wilderness area, so he sought to change the subject.

"Did you see any traffic pass by here today, Nix?"

"Just a couple of ranch trucks and one big white SUV. All of them were headed north," replied Nix.

"How many people in the SUV," asked Swifty.

"I couldn't tell. The SUV had all the windows tinted dark, and you couldn't see inside."

"Have you heard a weather forecast, Nix?" asked Kit.

"I got one this morning and had it downloaded from my satellite phone to the printer."

"You have a printer for your satellite phone?"

"Well, of course. How else would I be able to post copies of the weather report on the bulletin board on the front porch of the station?"

"Technology continues to amaze me," said Swifty. "Who knew?"

"So what is the weather forecast, Nix?"

"Weather looks good for tomorrow, but a cold front is moving in the next day, and it could bring thunderstorms or it could bring snow up above 7,000 feet."

"How much snow?"

"It would vary from location and altitude, but the range is from 10 to 22 inches and some strong winds to boot. Could be blizzard conditions above 8,000 feet."

"Well it sounds like rain down here and cooler weather in two days, but we can set up a tent we have or just camp out in the truck."

"If it does get bad you guys are welcome to stay with me in the station," said Nix.

"We just might take you up on that offer," replied Kit.

Nix helped Kit clean up the breakfast remains while Swifty re-stocked the pack mule. By the time Nix and Kit were done, Swifty was ready to leave. Kit mounted his horse and he and Swifty waved good-by to Nix as they turned their horses towards Trail Creek.

They rode southeast from the Dutch Joe Guard Station and soon were on a clear trail on the bank of Trail Creek. They followed the same trail that they had used the previous day. After about an hour they came to the junction with Squaw Creek.

They turned the horses north on the trail by Squaw Creek, and in about half an hour they were almost to the spot where Squaw Creek split into three separate forks when Swifty held up his hand in the halt signal.

"What is it?"

"I smell food cooking," said Swifty.

The two men dismounted and slowly led their horses as they approached the three way fork of Squaw Creek.

As they rounded a bend in Squaw Creek they could see a campsite about fifty yards ahead. A green dome tent had been pitched on a grassy area about twenty yards from the creek. As they got closer they could see a man and a woman sitting on some nearby rocks while they were working with a small propane stove. The aroma of bacon cooking was strong in the morning air.

"Howdy," said Swifty and the couple seemed to jump up in the air in surprise.

They quickly regained their composure and each of them said, "Good morning," to Swifty and Kit.

The two men tied off their horses on some nearby willow trees and walked forward and shook hands with the man and woman.

"I'm Kit Andrews and this is my partner, Swifty Olson."

The man was actually more of a boy. Kit judged him to be about mid-twenties and the girl a little younger.

They were both blonde and blue eyed and both were of average height and build and had an athletic look to them.

"I'm Troy Calhoun and this is my wife, Vicki Calhoun. Welcome to our little camp."

Kit noticed there was no evidence of any horses. "Are you folks backpackers?"

"That would be us," said Troy.

"We are on the second day of a week long trek up into the Wind River Mountains."

"You've got good weather for this early in the season. I hope it lasts for you."

"We've had a lot of experience backpacking, but this is our first trip to Wyoming. We chose this area because of its reputation for a sparse population. We were getting tired of hiking in areas that were always overcrowded with hikers and backpackers."

"Well, that shouldn't be a problem out here. Overcrowded in Wyoming would be an oxymoron."

All four of them laughed at Kit's attempt at a joke.

"Would you like to join us for some breakfast," asked Vicki as she spoke for the first time.

"We've already had our breakfast, but thank you just the same, ma'am."

"Sorry we interrupted your meal, but we're burning daylight and we've got to get moving," said Swifty as he walked over to the willows and retrieved their horses.

Both men mounted their horses and continued on their journey along Squaw Creek, each turning to wave good-bye to their new acquaintances.

About ten minutes later they came to the three way fork of Squaw Creek. They splashed across Squaw Creek and came up on the bank of the east side of the middle fork of Squaw Creek and followed the trail in the northeasterly direction.

The trail was wider and less rocky and twisted than the trail they had used the previous day following the west fork of Squaw Creek.

They made pretty good time, but the trail slowly became steeper and the temperature became somewhat cooler.

After about an hour, they stopped and let the horses water in the creek while they each took drinks of water out of their canteens.

"What did you make of the two backpackers?" asked Kit.

"I seriously doubt they are experienced backpackers."

"What makes you say that?"

"All of their gear, including their clothing, looked like it was brand new. The creases on their pants even had creases. I don't think their hiking boots were even close to being broken in."

"Anything else?"

"They are obviously greenhorns. Why would they lie to us?"

"It seemed to be that far from being surprised, they were expecting us."

"They were expecting us?"

"Yep. And I expect we'll see them again, although they may not want us to be able to see them."

"So they are not what they appear. You don't think they might be in the employ of some treasure hunting outfit, do you Kit?"

"I'd bet my next beer on it."

"At least we know who's trying to keep an eye on us."

"I doubt they are the only team in the field. This trip is liable to come up with some more unlikely surprises," said Kit.

*   *   *

Two hours later the trail had become much more difficult and began to compare all too well with the trail they had followed on the west fork the previous day. There were times when they could not see or even hear the water rushing down-hill in the middle fork of Squaw Creek.

The trail got narrower and more difficult as they climbed higher. The wind also seemed to increase in intensity. The middle fork of Squaw creek seemed to get smaller and smaller. Finally the trail crossed the creek at a point where the creek was less than a yard wide. Fifteen minutes later they both halted their horses and stared down at a small spring at the base of a very large boulder.

"This looks like where the middle fork begins," said Kit.

"There's no water on the upside of this boulder. The creek must start with this little spring."

"Let's walk the horses for a spell and try to find a place where we can get up higher and see if we can find any suitable snow fields."

"Sounds like a plan to me," said Swifty.

Both men dismounted and Swifty waited with the horses as Kit walked in half circles looking for a good trail that would lead them safely up the mountain.

Kit found a game trail and followed it uphill for about fifteen minutes. Satisfied that it would take them where he wanted to go, he returned to Swifty and they set out leading their horses.

"Kit, how about that spot?"

Kit looked up and to where Swifty was pointing. A small plateau seemed to jut out from the side of the mountain and looked like it would give them an unobstructed view of their surroundings from a point above them.

They made their way over to the plateau. It seemed to be made out of one giant rock sticking out of the side of the mountain. The huge rock extended out about thirty yards. Kit and Swifty tied their horses to some aspen trees and Swifty carefully made his way slowly out onto the plateau rock. He kept pausing to make sure the plateau was solidly anchored into the mountain and with each step he made out onto the large rock, he could feel no movement and no vibration. He made his way back to Kit who handed him the binoculars and the topographical map.

"You're not coming out there with me?" he asked Kit.

"I may be slow, but I'm not stupid. The rock may be fine with one of us, but who knows what happens with two of us. I'm not in favor of pushing our luck. You'll be fine out there alone."

"God, you're such a wuss. Afraid of a giant rock rolling down the side of a mountain for a few thousand feet."

"I bow to your obvious bravery or stupidity. I'm never sure which it is."

Swifty snorted in derision and made his way back out onto the rock plateau. Once he was near the edge he turned and used the binoculars to carefully scan the mountain above them with slow left to right patterns.

He let the binoculars drop to his chest, held onto his body by the strap around his neck. Then he took the map out of his back pocket and opened it up. He pulled a pen from his shirt pocket and made several notes on the map. He put the pen and map away and carefully made his way back across the plateau to where Kit was standing.

"Find anything useful?" asked Kit.

"I think I can see three fields that might be possibilities. They look to be a little bigger than the ones we saw yesterday so we need to get moving. I think we'll be doing more walking than riding so maybe we should change boots."

"I agree," said Kit.

They changed from cowboy boots to hiking boots and reloaded the pack horse.

They started to mount their horses when Kit paused and then dismounted.

"Give me the binoculars, Swifty."

"What for?"

"I need to look at something else."

Swifty handed the binoculars to Kit who promptly went out on the plateau and moved to the edge where he pulled up the binoculars and began to scan the area below them using the same side to side pattern that Swifty had used. After about two minutes he walked back to the horses, handed the binoculars to Swifty and mounted his horse.

"What was that all about?"

"I thought I might check to see if we were being followed."

"Are we being followed?"

"They aren't making very good time, but Biff and Muffy are right behind us."

Swifty laughed. "Those two are going to have sore and blistered feet by tonight. It serves them right."

They slowly rode their horses, as they followed the game trail.

When the trail became too narrow or too steep, they dismounted and led their horses.

After half an hour, they stopped for a water break and examined the marks on the topographical map Swifty had made.

"The first field should be just ahead, if your marks are right."

"My marks are always right."

"Of course they are. How dare I suggest otherwise," laughed Kit.

Soon they came to the edge of a long and fairly wide snowfield nestled along the side of the mountain. They broke out their snow shoes and began their slow pattern of searching in the soft snow.

They crossed the field horizontally at five yard intervals and then they did the same thing vertically. An hour later they had found nothing.

"Well that was fun," said Swifty. "Do we get extra travel points for snow shoe miles?"

"That's very funny. Where's the next field?"

Swifty pulled out the topographical map, looked to the east side of the mountain and promptly said, "Over there."

The next snow field was only about a quarter mile away, and it was smaller than the first. Again they donned their snow shoes and began their slow steady march across the snow. They walked for almost two hours and again found nothing.

After they removed and repacked the snow shoes, they decided to break for lunch. Swifty fed the horses some oats in feed bags made out of gunny sacks while Kit pulled out their pre-made lunch.

Kit used the small propane stove to make coffee and they sat around it on flat rocks and ate ham and cheese sandwiches. Dessert was an apple washed down with water from their canteens.

"I wonder what the dude and dudette are having for lunch?"

"I'm sure it's elegant and tasty. Something to go suitably with the blisters on their feet," laughed Kit.

*   *   *

"Goddamn my feet hurt" said the young blonde man, whose real name was Sam.

"That salesman lied to us about these boots being already broken in when they are new," replied the blonde woman whose real name was April.

They had stopped by the side of the narrow trail in the shade of some large boulders. Both of them sat on flat rocks and after removing their boots and socks, were examining their damaged feet.

April opened her backpack and pulled out a small first aid kit. She rummaged around for what she needed. Satisfied with what she found, she applied ointment to her feet and then added moleskin bandages.

"Here, Sam, put this on your feet."

"What is it?"

"The only relief we're going to get for our feet."

April put the kit back in her backpack and pulled out a fresh pair of wool socks and a pair of slightly used tennis shoes. She carefully pulled on the socks and then the tennis shoes. She picked up the despised boots and tossed them up into a pile of nearby rocks. "Have you ever heard of back-up?" she said.

Sam scowled at her as he pulled a fresh pair of socks out of his backpack and carefully worked them on over his bandaged feet. Finally he carefully pulled on his boots. As a final test he gingerly got slowly to his feet and took a couple of tentative steps.

"How does it feel?" asked April.

"Sore, but I can live with it."

"You're going to have to live with it, pal. There's no shoe store out here."

"You don't have to remind me. I knew this deal was a bad idea."

"It's not so bad. I prefer a healthy outdoors job than working in some rat-infested slum."

"I'm a city boy and I'll take the slum and the rats. At least there I know my way around. Out here there is lots and lots of nothing. Everything looks the same. No wonder nobody lives here."

"Nobody lives here because this is a designated wilderness area. Not only can't you live here, you can't have any motorized vehicles either. So it's horses or walking to get around."

"What time is it?"

April held out her arm and showed Sam her watch.

"Crap, I'm fifteen minutes late."

Sam dug into his backpack and came out with one of the latest and most expensive models of a satellite phone.

He fiddled with the controls and then waited for a satellite connection. When he was sure he had a good connection he dialed a pre-arranged phone number.

"Hello Control. This is Beta One."

"Yes, I read you four by four."

"I know I'm late in calling, but this isn't New York City."

"Yes, we intercepted the target and made contact this morning. We've been following them since."

"No, we've kept well behind them and haven't been made."

"No, I was not able to put a tracker on their horses or on either of them."

"I had no opportunity. They only stopped for a short while and never let us get close to them."

"I don't think we'll need the tracker. There's no one else out here and you can see for a long way. I can't see how we could lose them."

"Yes, we'll maintain distance and call in on the schedule unless something happens."

"I understand. Beta One out."

Sam shut off the phone and placed it back in his back pack. He sat back down on a flat rock with a worried look on his face.

"What's wrong?"

"That didn't go so well. Control is pissed that I didn't get a tracker on them or their horses."

"I could see you were having trouble, so I tried to distract them, but they weren't having any."

"To tell you the truth, I hesitated because those are two tough looking dudes. That one who was in the Delta Force has the eyes of a stone cold killer. He scared the shit out of me."

"There was nothing to be afraid of. They don't suspect us of anything. They aren't hardened criminals, just two very tough guys."

"If you read the report on them that I did you should know they aren't just tough, they're dangerous. Did you see their weapons? Those guys look more like bear hunters than deer hunters. I'm getting paid to observe and report, not get into a fire fight with Seal Team Six."

"Look, our job is to track and observe them and report if we see that they have found something. If they are lucky enough to find something, then we call in the heavyweights and we get the hell out of here because our job is done."

"Somehow I think you are making this sound a lot easier than it's going to be. Messing with those two can only mean trouble."

"I don't know about you, but I plan to stay out of trouble's way. Besides, we have done nothing to them."

"I don't think they are going to pause to figure that out if things go wrong."

"You're overreacting. There's not much that could go wrong if we do this right. We just stay out of their way."

CHAPTER FIFTEEN

Kit climbed up on a rock and stood completely still. He let his eyes slowly do a 360 degree scan of his surroundings. Then he closed his eyes and listened carefully, and he let his nose take in all the smells that were contained in the slight breeze.

He took inventory as he sat there. He could hear the wind in the nearby trees and a few birds singing downwind of their position. He could smell some sagebrush in the breeze and when he opened his eyes he could see no movement or anything around them that seemed out of place or unnatural.

Satisfied that they were not near any new danger, he got off the rock and walked over to Swifty.

Swifty had his topographical map spread out on the ground and was checking his marks.

"Find anything interesting?"

"It looks like we have one more smaller snowfield to check and then we need to head back down to camp," said Swifty.

"Lead the way. The sooner we get this field done, the better."

The two men led their horses for almost a mile, as Swifty used his compass for direction. Finally they cleared a line of ragged rocks and there was the snow field just below them.

Once again they donned snow shoes and began to walk a predicted pattern across the soft snow. Once Swifty held up his hand to halt their progress and he knelt down in the snow, but he came up with a small dark batch of leaves and nothing else. They returned to their pattern and once again they came up with nothing.

"Let's call it a day," said Kit.

"I'm voting in favor of your motion," replied Swifty. "I've walked in so many patterns today that I'm starting to walk cock-eyed."

Kit laughed and he repacked their snowshoes on the pack horse.

Within minutes they were leading their horses back down the trail the way they had come until they picked up what Swifty was sure was the main trail they had originally followed to get to the first of the three snow fields. After a couple of miles they were able to mount their horses and ride slowly down the trail.

Swifty held up his hand to halt their progress. He pulled his binoculars out of his saddle bag and sat motionless in the saddle with only his head swiveling as he moved the glasses back and forth horizontally for about 180 degrees in front of him.

After about five minutes, he slipped the binoculars back into the saddle bags and resumed their downward trek.

"See anything?"

"Our two intrepid backpackers are attempting to hide from us."

"Where are they?"

"Don't look, but they are about one hundred yards to your nine o'clock, about fifty yards below us."

"How did you see them?"

"I didn't. I smelled them. Close your eyes, take a deep breath, let it out and then smell. One of them has a weakness for garlic."

"At least they won't have to worry about vampires."

"From what I've seen of those two, vampires might be a blessing."

They continued down the mountain trail. The lower they got the better the trail got and they made even better time.

"I'm starting to wonder about that weather report we got from Nix."

"What about the report?"

"I haven't seen any sign of a change in the weather. There's hardly a cloud in the sky."

"Things can happen pretty fast in the mountains. A storm can appear and be on you in minutes. You're more likely to smell or feel the change in the air before you will see a forming storm."

"Just the same, I hope that weather report is wrong."

"Me too."

It was just turning to dusk when they rode into their camp by the Dutch Joe Guard Station. Nix was setting on the front porch on an old log bench, and he rose to wave to them.

"Any luck?" he asked.

"If it wasn't for bad luck we wouldn't have any luck at all," responded Swifty.

"That's too bad."

"Actually it's a reminder that this is a huge undertaking and we're trying to find a needle in a haystack in a huge field of haystacks," said Kit.

"Well, tomorrow's another day. See you at breakfast, Nix?"

"I wouldn't miss it. Can I bring anything?"

"Just bring your appetite."

"That's never a problem."

Swifty unsaddled the horses and unloaded the pack horse while Kit worked on rustling up some supper. When

Swifty had finished rubbing down the horses and fitting their feed bags on, he brought three buckets of water over to where the horses were hobbled. When the horses had finished their oats, Swifty took off the burlap feed bags and all three horses drank greedily from the buckets.

Swifty made another trip to the camp's well and washed the days grit and grim off of his hands and face.

He dipped his neckerchief in the cold water and tied it around his neck to help cool his body off.

Kit's supper special was homemade chili with a plain salad and some heated rolls with butter and honey. Coffee and ice water topped off the meal.

Kit cleaned up the dishes and Swifty checked on the horses and began to pack items for their journey up the east fork of Squaw Creek the next morning.

Twenty minutes later the camp was dark and quiet, the silence broken only by the occasional snoring of one of the dead-tired men.

*   *   *

"This stuff is disgusting," said April as she looked warily at what Sam had placed on her plate for supper. "What the hell is it?"

"These are called RME's. They're what the military eats. That's short for meals ready to eat."

"Ready to eat my ass," said April. "This stuff looks terrible and tastes even worse than it looks."

"Hey, it's food and it's hot. Don't complain. We're not out here to have gourmet meals. We're here to spy on those two cowboys and let our boss know if and when they actually find something up here in this god-forsaken wilderness."

When they had finished their meal, Sam and April pulled their sleeping bags nearer to the small campfire to share in the heat.

"I think it's getting colder," said April.

"Really. What was your first clue. Let me guess. You're losing the feeling in your feet."

"It's more like my fingers, but then my feet are fine in their comfortable shoes, unlike someone else I know."

"I changed the bandages on my feet and they seem to be okay, but they are sore. I hope those two cowboys find something in one of these snowfields, so we can sit tight and watch them without having to hike all day."

"Somehow that seems too good to be possibly true," said April.

Soon, both of the greenhorn backpackers were sound asleep.

CHAPTER
SIXTEEN

Swifty was up at dawn repacking items on the pack horse. Kit had breakfast ready and Nix came out of the ranger station just in time to sit down to eat.

"Timing is everything, young Mr. Nix," said Swifty.

"Being in time for breakfast is being just in time to me," he replied.

"What's the plan for today?" asked Nix.

"We start searching the forks of the east fork of Squaw Creek. According to the map there are several forks. I think I counted five, but I can't be sure with this map."

"Will you search them all today?" asked Nix.

"No. This time we'll camp up in the mountains because it may take us three days to search this fork. It covers a lot bigger area."

"You'll have to fend for yourself for breakfast tomorrow morning, Nix," laughed Swifty.

"I'll manage," said an obviously disappointed Nix.

"We may call you on the satellite phone for a weather update. Will that be okay?" asked Kit.

"Of course it will. I'll look forward to your call."

Nix and Kit cleaned up the breakfast dishes and by the time they were done, Swifty had the horses ready and the pack horse loaded up. He and Kit mounted their horses and with a wave to Nix they were headed down the trail to Trail Creek.

Soon they reached the junction with Squaw Creek, and they headed northwest until they came to the three forks. This time they took the eastern fork of Squaw Creek and they made good time for about an hour with a good wide trail that looked pretty well traveled.

Swifty called a halt and they both dismounted. Swifty motioned to Kit to have him come next to Swifty so he could show him something on the trail. When Kit got next to him, Swifty whispered, "We got company."

"Where?" whispered Kit back.

"They're about fifty yards above us and about seventy yards to the east."

Kit stood and without looking in the direction that Swifty had indicated, he listened and attempted to smell his surroundings.

"Do you hear them?" whispered Swifty.

"No, but I can sure smell them. They really are tenderfeet," Kit whispered back.

The two remounted their horses and continued on up the rocky trail. The trail was fairly broad and was next to the right bank of the creek.

As they climbed higher on the trail they began to see more small trails of water around them. Each small trail of water came from melting snow and ice above them and each trail made its way down hill in a roundabout fashion to finally merge with the creek. They also began to see small pockets of colorful wildflowers. Kit was especially fond of the bright orange-red color of the Indian paint brush.

They came to a point where the creek forked to the northwest, away from the northerly track of their trail.

Swifty found an easy ford, and they crossed the creek and started up the newly found fork on the northerly side where a faint game trail was evident

Less than an hour later, they came to the source of the small fork and there were no snow fields visible to them. They retraced their steps and soon were back at the junction of the fork and Squaw Creek. They re-crossed Squaw Creek and found their original trail and began to ride north along the east bank of the creek.

As they continued north the trail became steeper, more rocky, and much more difficult. After almost an hour, they stopped for a break and watered their horses in the creek.

Both Kit and Swifty sat on nearby rocks, closed their eyes and focused on what they could hear and smell.

After about a minute, both men opened their eyes and looked around.

"Get anything?" asked Swifty.

"Nothing, unless you count the sagebrush, the small song birds, and that small Pika over by you."

"Pika? Where? I don't see one."

"That little mouse like critter to your left."

Swifty looked left and sure enough, there staring at him from his entrance in a pile of rocks about five feet away was a Pika standing on his hind legs.

Swifty took a step in the direction of the rocks and the Pika quickly dove down his entrance to his rock home and disappeared from sight.

"He's certainly a good judge of character," said Kit with a grin.

"He's just another stupid mouse," said Swifty.

"He's smart enough to stay away from the likes of you," hooted Kit.

"Yeah, yeah, he's probably a male and rightfully afraid of me."

"And if the Pika was female?"

"She'd be sitting in my hand, totally infatuated with me."

"Swifty, if bullshit were music, you'd be a brass band."

Swifty made a face at Kit and quickly mounted his horse. Kit followed and soon both men were heading higher on the steep and narrow trail.

They came to where the creek forked to the right, heading northeast, and they followed the fork, staying on the east bank. There was not much of a trail, but what existed was a little more level and less steep and narrow, and they made good time. Soon they came to a place where the creek had widened into a good sized pond, and they stopped to have lunch.

"I wonder what caused the pond," said Kit.

Swifty pointed to a spot on the other size of the pond that looked like a mound of small wood sticks. "Beaver," he said.

Sure enough, a beaver dam had been built about a hundred yards upstream of the fork and the hump they were looking at was the roof of the beaver lodge.

They watered the horses and then hobbled them while the two men ate their lunch.

"Ham and cheese sandwiches. Food fit for a king," announced Kit who had made their lunch up that morning.

"It'll do," said Swifty as he wolfed down his first sandwich.

Neither man spoke as they consumed their lunch and carefully took in all their surroundings. Kit could see that the fork of the creek continued on almost the same northeasterly direction and in the distance it seemed to drop slightly to the south.

Lunch completed, they mounted their horses and continued on along the creek. They soon passed the east end of the beaver pond and after about a mile, the creek and their path seemed to take a hard right to the south for a few hundred yards and then headed northeasterly again.

The trail became a little steeper, but still quite passable, and after another hour they came to the source of the creek's fork. A small spring seemed to bubble up from beneath a large pile of rocks. They brought their horses to a stop and Swifty dismounted and handed his reins to Kit.

Swifty grabbed his binoculars from his saddle bag and began to climb up the pile of rocks above the spring. When he had reached the top of the rock pile he stood and slowly scanned the area around them with particular attention to the north of their position. Seemingly satisfied, Swifty carefully made his way down the rock pile and after securing his binoculars, he took the reins from Kit and mounted his horse.

"See anything?"

"I see lots of rocks and sagebrush and not much else. There are a few small snowfields, but they're not big enough to contain a Volkswagen, let along the debris field of a crashed airplane."

"That doesn't sound very promising."

"It certainly didn't look promising, either. Let's head back to Squaw Creek and find something with more potential."

"You lead on, Swifty. I'll bring up the rear."

The trail going back to the east fork of Squaw Creek was in good shape and not difficult so they made good time and soon where letting their horses water in the creek.

"The creek and the game path are headed north, so I guess we are too."

"My guess is our snowfields are likely higher up to the north," said Swifty.

"Let's head out," said Kit.

The two men pulled on their reins and got their horses heads out of the creek water and headed north.

Once again they began to see small rivulets of water created by the melting snow of the higher elevations and flowing down until they joined with the creek. Wildflowers began to appear in abundance and what grasses there were seemed to shine with colors that almost appeared to be emerald green.

The trail gradually became steeper and their pace slowed accordingly. They saw rabbits and an occasional fox as they made their way steadily up the mountainside under the watchful eye of a golden eagle overhead who seemed to float in endless circles above them.

Suddenly Swifty put up his right hand to signal a stop. Without uttering a sound, he dismounted and threw the reins of his horse to Kit and after placing a finger over his mouth in a sign of silence, Swifty disappeared into the nearby brush.

Kit remained motionless on his horse. He carefully scanned his surroundings. He could see nothing out of the ordinary, and he could hear nothing but the wind and an occasional songbird. The wind shifted and then his nose told him why Swifty had stopped.

Kit wasn't sure what he smelled, but he knew it wasn't natural. It almost smelled like a perfume, but he knew that wasn't possible.

Swifty appeared suddenly out of the brush where he had originally disappeared. He walked up to Kit and took the reins to his horse. Standing next to Kit, he spoke so softly that Kit had to strain to hear what he was saying.

"We have company up ahead of us on the trail. Looks like a lady forest ranger on horseback. She's just sitting on a rock by the creek with her horse tied off to a pine tree. It almost looks like she's expecting us."

"So, what's the plan?"

"We ride up and act surprised. But keep your gun handy. I have a sincere dislike of coincidences."

Kit grinned and headed his horse up the side of the creek, while Swifty mounted his horse and quickly followed.

In about fifteen minutes they followed the creek as it turned around some large rocks and then they could see her about fifty yards up ahead of them.

As they rode nearer, Kit made her out to be a woman in her forties, but in very good physical shape. She had gray hair pulled back in a pony-tail. She had light grey eyes. She was wearing a uniform just like Ranger Nix, except she was wearing a Smokey the Bear hat and he did not recall ever seeing Nix wearing one.

Upon seeing their approach, she stood up from her perch on the rock and waited for them with her hands on her hips.

Both men reined in their horses at a respectful distance and each of them touched the brim of their cowboy hats in greeting.

"Howdy, ma'am," said Swifty. Kit greeted the lady ranger as well.

"Hello, boys," she said. "What brings you up to the Wind Rivers?"

"Actually we're looking for somebody," said Kit.

"I didn't see anyone camping up behind me and I just came down from Little Sandy Creek. Is this someone who's lost?"

"Well, he's sort of lost, at least to us."

"What do you mean by that?"

"I mean we're looking for someone who crash landed in an airplane in 1928."

"1928! Well I'd say he's been lost a very long time," she said with a hint of a smile."

Kit had been studying her and even in her forties, she was still a pretty attractive woman. Her uniform looked like it had been tailor made and he could see no smudges of dirt or hint of much in the way of wrinkles on her clothes.

"Pardon our lack of manners, ma'am. My name is Kit Andrews and this is my partner Swifty Olson."

She extended her right hand as she said, "I'm U.S. Forest Ranger Patricia Greenway, but you can call me Pat."

They shook hands all around and then ranger Greenway said, "Are you really looking for an eighty year old plane wreck or are you just pulling my leg?"

Kit smiled at her and went on to explain what had happened to the Air Mail flight from Rock Springs so many years ago.

"My lord, that's quite a story. How did you happen to wind up here next to Squaw Creek?"

"We have a few bits and pieces of information and this is one of the places that seem to fit with some of the information."

"So you're not sure that this is the right place," she said."

"That's right," Kit replied. "The crash site could be in any number of places and even if we knew exactly where he crashed, that doesn't mean we would be able to find him."

"Then hunting for the crash site could take a very long time," Pat said.

"Obviously we might never find the site and even then we might never find the pilot's remains, but we think it's worth a try."

"Time doesn't really matter to the site," said Swifty. "Old man Hopper's not going anywhere."

Both Kit and Pat laughed at Swifty's remark.

"Well I don't want to keep you boys from your job. Good luck with your search."

"Good luck to you too, ma'am," said Kit and he and Swifty rode past her and continued north along the east side of the creek.

CHAPTER SEVENTEEN

After riding for half an hour, Swifty called a halt and he and Kit dismounted while they let the horses water in the creek. Kit took some jerky out of a pouch in his jacket pocket and then tossed the pouch to Swifty who helped himself to some jerky and tossed the pouch back to Kit. Kit took a swig of water from his canteen and looked back down the trail.

"Something is not right with that ranger lady," he said.

"I second that, but what makes you say that?"

"If she had been up on the trail by the divide on Little Sandy Creek and then come down this side her outfit wouldn't look like she was doing a camera shoot in a fashion magazine. She is the first ranger I ever saw with long painted fingernails. Her horse didn't have a government brand and her rig was not government-issue. She never asked us about reporting whatever we found to the Forest Service or making any kind of a report. She never asked us for any identification. If she's a ranger I'm the Easter bunny."

"Well, your ears are kinda long. You could be at least part bunny."

Kit ignored his partner's remarks and turned back to look up the trail. "How many more of these phonies are we going to run into going up this creek?"

"I imagine as many as they need to keep track of us. Let's face it. Nothing is going to happen until we actually find something of value that they want."

"Then we better work on a plan on what to do when that happens."

"Works for me. Let's think on it while we ride and discuss it when we set up camp tonight," said Swifty.

Kit nodded and both men mounted their horses and headed upstream with Kit in the lead.

*   *   *

The lady ranger who called herself Patricia Greenway resumed her seat on the flat rock while her horse munched away at the sparse, but green and tasty grass near her.

After almost forty minutes she heard noises on the trail below her and her hand slipped down to the holstered pistol at her side.

Within ten minutes the two bedraggled backpackers walked into her view. They seemed surprised to see her, and she smiled to herself as she realized they thought she was a real ranger.

"You two must be April and Sam. Am I correct?"

"What did you say?" mumbled a shocked Sam.

"You heard me. I'm your field contact on this project. I got your message about your shoe issues and decided to contact you."

"My feet are killing me," said Sam. April said nothing but if looks could kill, Sam would be six feet under.

"Try these," said Greenway as she pulled a pair of heavy duty tennis shoes out of her saddle bags and tossed them to the ground in front of Sam.

"Oh, wow," said Sam as he retrieved the shoes. "These are my size." He immediately sat down in the dirt and carefully took off his hiking boots and then slipped on the new tennis shoes. He tentatively stood up and took a couple of steps. "Oh, this is so much better. I don't know how to thank you."

"Don't worry about it. It's coming out of your paycheck."

"I don't care. Whatever they cost it's worth it."

April looked at Sam with total disgust. She couldn't believe she had been teamed up with such a weenie.

"Do you have any new instructions for us?" she asked Greenway.

"You're to continue to keep the subjects in visual sight and report daily to Control," answered Greenway.

"That'll be a lot easier to do when my feet aren't killing me," said Sam.

"Where will you be?" April asked Greenway.

"I'll be around keeping an eye on you keeping an eye on the subjects."

"Who else is up here keeping an eye on those two cowboys?" asked Sam.

"That is none of your business, Sam. I can tell you that we're not alone, but you, like the two cowboys will be unaware of any others presence until the crash site is located."

"Got it," said a sullen Sam.

Without another word, Greenway mounted her horse and rode away from the two backpackers in an easterly direction.

*   *   *

Kit and Swifty came to another fork of the creek and this one extended from the east joining with the east fork of Squaw Creek from a northeasterly direction.

Without pausing Kit guided his horse to the right bank of the newly found fork and Swifty followed.

The trail next to the fork was almost non-existent and finally disappeared until their only guide was staying on the right bank of the creek.

The land began to rise and become steeper and the creek became narrower. Kit called a halt and after watering the horses, he and Swifty began walking and leading their horses along the side of the creek.

As they walked along the creek bank, the creek took a hard turn to the right until it was almost coming from the southeast. As they made the turn they surprised a small herd of mule deer. The deer quickly turned and bounded out and through the sagebrush until they were out of sight.

After another fifteen minutes of walking, they had reached the source of the creek. It was another spring that seemed to come up from under a large rock formation that jutted out from the mountain for about fifty yards.

They tied off their horses and Swifty began to climb up the rock formation until he reached a height he felt was satisfactory and then he pulled out his binoculars, and slowly turned as he scanned the area above them and to the east and west. Apparently satisfied, he put away the binoculars and carefully climbed down off the rocks.

"See anything?"

"There are snowfields way up above us, but I can't tell how big or how long they are because I can only see part of them from here. They may be the fields we're looking for, but I can't tell until I can get above them or even with them."

Kit looked up at the clouds in the sky and then looked at his watch.

"This looks like a good place to camp and we can get an early start in the morning. We need to head back to the east fork of Squaw Creek and keeping heading up the mountain."

"I agree. This place will do just fine."

Swifty unsaddled the horses and led them to the creek to water them. Kit had unloaded the pack horse and began pulling what he needed out of the packs.

By the time Swifty had watered and fed the horses Kit had started a small fire and begun preparing their supper. Within twenty minutes they sat down in the dirt to a hot meal of beans, bacon, fried potatoes, and hot coffee.

After supper Kit cleaned up the dishes and cookware and repacked them and unpacked their sleeping bags and a flask of brandy. Kit handed him a metal cup of hot coffee

"Oh, that's good," said Swifty as he sipped from the hot metal cup. "Keep this up and someday you'll make some guy a great wife."

Kit's response was to toss his now empty coffee cup at Swifty and watch it bounce off his back.

Swifty retrieved the cup along with his own and washed them out in the creek and then packed them up.

He returned to their campfire and sat down across the fire from Kit.

Kit was searching for something in his vest when a piece of paper came out and floated over the camp fire and landed next to Swifty.

"What's this," asked Swifty?

"It was in my mail when I stopped in the post office before we left Kemmerer."

Swifty looked the card over and said, "Who's it from?"

"I think it's from Conner."

"Didn't he sell his place and sort of disappear?"

"Yes, he did. He was always secretive and kind of cryptic so I'm pretty sure this is from him."

Swifty looked over the picture on the post card.

"So is he in Mexico or Hawaii?"

"I have no idea. My money would be on Mexico."

"Why Mexico?"

"It's closer and a lot cheaper and Conner is the kind of guy who throws quarters around like they were manhole covers."

Swifty laughed.

"Manhole covers. That's a good one."

"You've never talked much about your dad and what happened to him."

Kit looked at Swifty, then down at the fire and then back at Swifty.

"My dad left my mom when I was very young. Later my mom told me he was dead. I had no idea he was alive until I came to Kemmerer and found out from Big Dave and Woody."

"Have you ever seen him?"

"Only when I was very little, but I don't remember anything about him. I've never even seen a recent picture of him."

"So you have a dad who you've basically never seen and you're living in his house?"

"That's about the size of it. I did find pictures of me in various stages of growing up in his closet. How he got them I have no idea."

"That is strange."

Swifty got up to grab his sleeping bag from the pack horse.

By the time he returned to the small campfire, Kit was sound asleep in his sleeping bag.

"Slacker," said Swifty to an unhearing and uncaring Kit.

Then he slid into his sleeping bag and was quickly fast asleep.

*   *   *

Both men were up at dawn and after a quick breakfast and repacking they were on their way back down the creek fork. Dawn showed an overcast sky and a decided drop in the temperature.

They made good time retracing their path down the east bank of the creek and a slowly growing wind seemed to help hurry the horses along.

Once they reached the place where the fork regained the left fork of Squaw Creek, they dismounted and watered their horses. When the horses were satisfied, they tied them off to a small grove of willow trees and sat down on some flat rocks. Kit tossed the sack of jerky and a canteen to Swifty and soon both of them were chewing on jerky and looking anxiously at the growing cloud banks to the northwest of them.

"I don't like the looks of those clouds," said Swifty.

"The wind is getting stronger here and you can bet it's plenty strong up there. It's likely the wind will blow those clouds right over us."

"Always the optimist. This time I hope you're right."

"Well, we can always look forward to seeing whoever or whatever has been sent out to spy on us. It's becoming a daily occurrence."

"Are you sure that lady ranger was a spy. She wasn't bad looking for a gal in her forties."

"If I'm an optimist then you are the worst judge of character in Wyoming."

Swifty just laughed.

"A whole lot of people have wasted a lot of time and money if we don't find this crash site."

"Well, there is no guarantee we'll find anything except for more snow and rocks and there's a lot of that up here."

"I don't think these folks are going to be very happy with us if we come empty handed."

"Last time I checked we weren't working for them," said Kit.

"Well, if we are, they're really slow with their paychecks."

"I don't think paychecks for us are in their plans."

"Just what the hell are their plans?"

"It's simple. They shadow us until we find something. Then they jump us and take it away from us. Let us do all the hard work and then they cash in."

"What if we don't want to be jumped?"

"Neither of us is planning on getting jumped. If we find this site, we're going to mark it on a GPS and then you and I are going to vanish and leave these poor saps wandering around in these mountains wondering what happened."

"Works for me. What happens if we can't ditch them?"

"We teach them that they picked the wrong two cowboys to mess with."

"That also works for me."

"Let's go. We're burning daylight."

"I believe that was John Wayne in the movie, (The Cowboys.)"

"You are correct. Let's move out."

Very quickly they were headed north on the east bank of the east fork of Squaw Creek. There wasn't much of a trail, but although the going was steep, the ground was rocky, but fairly even.

A hawk flew high over their heads as they made their way upstream, but they did not see any other wildlife. The sky above them grew darker and thicker with dark clouds.

Twice Swifty slipped off his horse and tossed his reins to Kit and then disappeared in the nearby brush on foot so he could scout both behind them and ahead of them. Each time he returned without comment. Kit knew that meant he had seen nothing of importance.

After almost two hours they came to a place where the creek split into two forks. One fork went to the east and then to the north and the other fork went to the west and then to the north. On the map it looked like two arms reaching out and then up. Creating the fork was a massive outcropping of the mountain in front of them. The outcropping seemed to go up forever and certainly it went up further than they could see.

The stone wall outcropping created in front of them was almost vertical. According to Kit's map the fork to the east looked like it headed to the northeast and then ended up around 11,000 feet and the fork to the west seemed to go northwest and then hooked to almost straight north and looked to end about 11,800 feet above sea level.

"All right fearless leader. Which way do we go?" asked Swifty.

"The last two forks we took were to the east. I say we try our luck with the fork to the west for a change of pace and hopefully our luck."

"We could always flip a coin," said Swifty.

"We could also look for a sign."

"A sign? What kind of sign?"

"A traffic sign, you moron."

"You're looking for a traffic sign, and I'm the moron?"

"Let's cross the creek and take the north side of the west fork."

Swifty just grinned at him and then turned his horse to the west and splashed across the creek and Kit quickly followed him. Swifty stopped after crossing the creek and turned his horse to face Kit.

"I think we ought to make a cache here."

"Why make a cache here?"

"Let's say we get up to near the top and find the site and the diamonds. They're going to nail us on the way down. Instead we could continue down to the east and catch the other eastern fork and follow it down. If something happens to us we at least have the cache no matter which way we come down."

"Swifty, that might be the brightest idea you've ever had."

They rode a short distance up both sides of the outcropping until Swifty found a small cave that was barely big enough for a small man to fold himself into. Swifty placed two pistols, ammo, survival blankets, a first aid kit and a bag of jerky in a bag in the cave and covered the entrance with small rocks and then brush. Taking out a small ice axe, he cut a cross in the rocks above the cave to mark the site. When he was finished, they both mounted their horses and continued up the west fork. While Swifty was satisfied with his work, Kit was not. He took out his GPS and took a reading of their location and entered it in the GPS as a waypoint.

They mounted their horses and resumed their journey upstream. Riding on the right bank of the creek was intimidating as just forty yards to Kit's right was the sheer vertical stone wall of the mountain towering high above him.

The creek continued to rise with the land and the creek bank, while even, was getting much steeper. The creek itself was getting smaller the higher they climbed, so Kit knew they were getting closer to the water's source.

Finally Swifty put up his hand to call a halt, and he then slid out of his saddle to the ground. Kit followed his lead and dismounted. They tied their horses off to some brush on the creek bank close enough to allow the horses to drink freely.

"This place is getting downright spooky," said Swifty."

"You mean the stone wall on our right that is blocking out the world?"

"That and how quiet it is. I haven't heard even a bird for half an hour. That's not natural."

"I wonder what the hell is up there?" said Kit. "I can't see the top of whatever this is."

"My guess is we're looking up at the edge of some glacier," said Swifty.'

"Glacier!" said Kit. "It's a glacier! That's it!"

"What the hell are you talking about, Kit?"

"Don't you remember when we asked that bald cowboy back at the ranch for directions to the crash site."

"You mean the cowboy named Curly?"

"Yes, Yes, Curly Polk. He was the one who told us what his pal Lew Cavanaugh told him about where he found the crash site."

"What did he say?"

"Let me check my notes I took on my iPhone," said Kit.

After getting his phone turned on and hitting a couple of icons, Kit found what he was looking for.

"He said Lew described the place as the south end of a long fairly narrow snow field elevated up several feet from the meadow. The snow field was just north of the head of the lower fork of Squaw Creek. He said there were five fingers running off Squaw Creek and this is the fourth of five forks of the creek!

"Is this the right fork?"

"He said it was the finger that runs mostly to the north that he followed to the snow field. He said that if you were to stand where he stood and looked up you'd be looking at the south edge of Knife's Edge glacier. He said Knife's Edge is a high narrow glacier at the very top of the south end of the Wind River Mountains and the glacier is very narrow at the top and the sides of the mountain there are very steep and very sheer. The glacier runs straight down both sides like a saddle on a skinny horse. I think this is it."

"This is it?"

"If I'm right, then the snow field has to be just up ahead of us. It's probably above the source of this creek."

Swifty remounted his horse and looked over at Kit.

"Let's go," said Swifty and he spurred his horse to move upstream and Kit quickly followed.

CHAPTER EIGHTEEN

It took them almost an hour of travel both riding and then on foot leading their horses before they came to the source of the creek. The creek had shrunken to the size of a trickle as it came out from under the rock wall of the mountain. Both men stopped to refill their canteens and let the horses drink their fill of the cold water.

Kit handed his reins to Swifty, and he walked up a small pinnacle of rocks that seemed to rise out of the ground. Once he was about twenty feet above the ground Kit stopped and used his binoculars to look up and ahead. He seemed to check the area twice and then he pocketed the binoculars and carefully descended the rock formation.

"What have we got?" asked Swifty.

Kit smiled. "We have a long and fairly wide snowfield that runs northwest to southeast and it starts about eight feet above the rock ground we're standing on."

"That sounds like the snowfield this Lew guy described."

"It certainly does. Let's go find out, Partner."

The snowfield was about half a mile away, and they quickly covered the distance over rocky ground interspersed with small rivulets of melting snow water and patches of brightly colored wildflowers.

Once they reached the snowfield, they led their horses to the north end where the field seemed to start. They hobbled the horses and unpacked their snowshoes.

They decided to walk around the perimeter of the snowfield and began to walk a now familiar grid. With each cycle of the grid, they moved closer to the middle of the field. The snow was soft and spongy and each of them occasionally slipped when the snow gave way beneath their snowshoes. They had made three complete trips around the snowfield when Swifty yelled out, "Hold it!"

"What've you got?" asked Kit.

"I'm not sure, but there is something dark just under the snow. Make your way over here and help me look."

Kit moved to his left and closed the ten yards that had been between them until he stood almost next to Swifty. He looked down to where Swifty was pointing. Sure enough, there was something there.

Swifty knelt on the snow and began to slowly pull the snow away with his gloved hands. Finally he reached down and slowly pulled up a piece of wood that was over two feet long. He looked it over and handed it up to Kit.

Kit looked carefully at the wood. It appeared to be a hardwood and was slightly curved and obviously hand crafted. Kit grinned.

"What is it?" asked Swifty.

"This, my friend is part of a wooden rib from a very old airplane. The fuselage and wings were fabric stretched over a skeleton of formed wood. This is part of the airplane's skeleton. Unless I am greatly mistaken, we just found the crash site of old Wild Bill Hopper."

They set up a new search grid using the site of the wooden rib as the hub of the grid. Within half an hour they had found more pieces of wood and a few rusted pieces of metal hardware that must have been fasteners of some kind.

About twenty yards in front of the hub they found about a third of a wooden propeller. Fifty yards further in front they found the rather large remains of a Ford Liberty 12 engine.

Kit touched Swifty on the shoulder and indicated that they should stand in front of the location of the engine and look back to the north to the location of the hub of their search.

"It appears that he landed from the north which seems strange because he would have been heading west and gotten blown off course."

"Maybe he saw the field and he turned around to try to use it to land?"

"That is a real possibility. Anyway, we know he landed somewhere around where we found the wood and the plane began to break up and the last thing left, and the heaviest, would be the engine which we just found. If I'm right, then everything is between us and the hub where we found the wood rib."

"Let's walk back from the engine to the hub at a five foot interval and then back to the engine with another five foot interval," said Swifty.

"Sounds like a plan."

They slowly made their way back toward the hub. Periodically they halted as they found more pieces of wood and metal. They also found another large piece of the propeller. Swifty found more pieces of rusted metal and several strands of rusted wires.

"Where's this fabric you were talking about?" asked Swifty.

"The fabric and leather and things like that are long gone to the elements," said Kit.

"Maybe they're not all gone. I see something below me that looks like some kind of leather," said Swifty.

He knelt in the snow and began digging with his hands. He changed positions to continue scooping up snow until he had a hole about a yard across and about three feet deep. Then he stopped.

"This looks like leather to me, Kit. I'm not sure exactly what it is, but . . . . holy shit!"

"What is it?"

"I think I found the pilot's leather helmet, and it's still attached to the pilot."

Kit rushed over and helped Swifty dig. They dug about four feet of snow up and sure enough there was the mummified remains of a frozen Wild Bill Hopping. He was in a sitting position and he was bent over like he had fallen asleep.

"My God. I never thought we'd actually find the old guy. What a hell of a way to die. What do we do now? How do we get him out of here?"

"We don't. We'll need to rebury him and mark the grave. The forest service will have to approve a helicopter to come up here and evacuate him."

"Should we move him?"

"We should probably not move him. We could maybe dig the hole deeper to help preserve him and then slide him into the deeper hole and cover him up with packed snow."

They took off their snow shoes and worked on their knees as they dug an even deeper hole next to the frozen corpse. When they were done they both knelt next to Wild Bill's body.

"Let's each grab a side and on the count of three we'll push him into the deeper hole."

"Fine with me."

"One, two, ..."

"Wait, wait. Hold it!"

"What's wrong?"

"Look at the front of his flight jacket!"

"What about his jacket?"

"He's got something in his jacket. It looks like some kind of metal box."

Kit moved closer to the body and looked carefully at the partially closed flight jacket. Sure enough, there was the end of a metal box about sixteen inches long and about eight inches wide and about three and a half inches deep.

"Hold him where he is and don't let him slip into the new hole," said Swifty.

Kit complied and did his best to maintain a grip on the frozen corpse.

Swifty slowly and carefully worked his gloved hand into the opening in the front of the flight jacket and just as slowly he withdrew it with the metal box in his grasp.

"Man, this thing is heavy for such a small box," said Swifty as he finally held the box in both hands.

"Would you say it weighed about ten pounds," asked a poker faced Kit.

"That sounds about right," said Swifty.

Swifty placed the box on the snow field and then he and Kit carefully slid the frozen body of Wild Bill Hopping into the new deeper hold they had dug. Then they covered the body with snow and packed it down.

Swifty and Kit each slid their snowshoes back on and Swifty walked back to the horses to find something to mark the grave with while Kit stayed by the grave site and the metal box. Kit took out his GPS and after he had acquired three satellites he got a longitude and latitude position for the grave site which he saved on the GPS unit as a waypoint.

Swifty returned with about a seven foot branch which he had trimmed with his knife. He pulled a red bandanna out of his hip pocket and tied it to the top of the pole. He started to push the branch into the snow when Kit stopped him.

"What's wrong?" asked Swifty.

"Maybe we don't want to mark the site. We're not exactly on some scientific expedition to excavate some historic site under some government permit. We're in the middle of a wilderness with some really nasty folks trying to keep tabs on us. Maybe we need to keep on looking over this field and not act like we found what we're looking for."

"You think we're being watched?"

"It's possible, although I think it would be hard to see us unless we could see them as well."

"Okay with me" said Swifty and he removed the bandanna and tossed the pole aside.

They resumed their walking pattern on the snowfield until they had covered the entire field.

Both men then walked back to the horses where they removed their snowshoes and Kit started a small fire to make coffee, while Swifty fed the horses.

When the coffee was made they each knelt by the fire and drank hot coffee while they stared at the mysterious box.

"I am going to assume that this is the box of diamonds that those women failed to mention to me," said Kit.

"One way to find out," said Swifty.

Swifty reached down and picked up the box. He examined it carefully. "The box has no markings and there is a small, but sturdy, and very rusted padlock on the box."

"Is that a problem?"

"Not for me," said Swifty. He proceeded to walk over to the packs and came back with a chisel and a small hammer. After three blows with the hammer the padlock was gone.

Swifty sat the box on the ground between them and carefully worked the top of the metal box open.

Neither man spoke. There in front of them were hundreds of polished diamonds, each of them flashing facets of captured sunlight.

"I've never seen anything like this."

"Me either," said Kit.

"How much do you think these suckers are worth?"

"I have no idea. All I know about diamonds is that women love them and men can't afford them."

"So who do they belong to?"

"Again, I have no idea. We found them on government land. When they were shipped, they were entrusted to the government mail system. I would guess they belong to whoever the heirs are to the folks who originally shipped them."

"Everybody involved with these diamonds including our buddy Wild Bill are all dead now."

"Speaking of dead, now that we've found Wild Bill and the diamonds, we could end up dead if we're not careful. All those folks who have been trying to keep track of us will be showing up real soon and I don't think they are likely to take no for an answer."

"Well, it's been a while since we've been in a real good fight," said Swifty.

"If it's a fight you want, I'm pretty sure they'll oblige you."

"We better get something more useful to carry these babies in than this beat up old box."

"I have a couple of pretty good canvas drawstring sacks in my saddlebags. We can split them up so each of us is carrying about five pounds.

"Sounds like a good idea," said Swifty as he rose to his feet and went over to Kit's horse and retrieved the bags. They filled the bags and each of them put a bag in their saddlebags. Swifty picked up the old metal box and walked back into the snowfield. He knelt down in the snow and dug a hole with his hands. When he was satisfied it was deep enough, he tossed the box into the hole and filled it in with packed snow.

When Swifty finished burying the box, he looked up to see Kit pulling his rifle, pistol, and a small cleaning kit out of a pack.

Swifty followed suit and after they had cleaned their weapons and reloaded them, Kit broke out a frying pan and proceeded to make a quick meal of beans and bacon along with a couple of thick hunks of bread.

Kit had just finished cooking when Swifty walked up carrying fleece jackets, heavy wool socks, their hiking boots, and their heavy cowboy slickers and wool knit caps and balaclavas.

"Weather's changing. Those nasty looking clouds to the west are headed our way in a hurry and things could get nasty. We should look for a place to hole up until this passes."

"Didn't the O.J. character tell us about some good sized caves around here? Let's get packed and then split up and see if we can find one."

"Good idea. Let's get packed."

They packed quickly and leaving the horses hobbled, each set out on foot after agreeing to be back within thirty minutes whether they found anything or not.

Kit walked carefully back the way they had come, and Swifty went past the snowfield to the east. After half an hour Kit had found nothing and the wind had continued to pick up. He could see the dark clouds in the west had gotten closer and much larger. He headed back so he would not be late and when he got back to the horses, Swifty was waiting for him.

"Did you find anything Kit?"

"Nope. Nothing we could use."

"Luckily for us Swifty has a nose for caves."

"You found one!"

"Actually I found two. Let's get moving."

They walked, leading their horses for about twenty minutes. The storm was suddenly upon them and the strong cold winds were accompanied with small hard snowflakes that quickly turned to sleet. They carefully led their horses and traveled in single file with Swifty in the lead. Very shortly Swifty signaled a halt, but with the wind and sleet Kit could not see Swifty and only knew they had stopped because he ran into Swifty's horse. Kit looked just past where his partner now stood. Sure enough Swifty had found a good sized cave that was five feet high, twenty feet deep and about ten feet wide. It was only about four feet wide at the mouth. He also found a cave that was more of an indentation in the rock that must have been carved out of the rock by some ancient river and wind. The indenture was ten feet high and eight feet deep and about twenty feet wide.

"This should work for the horses," said Kit.

"My thought exactly."

They unloaded the packs and saddlebags from the horses and stuffed everything into the first cave and left the saddled horses hobbled in the indenture.

While they were working the wind became much stronger and they could feel the temperature quickly getting much colder. By the time they had the horses secured and were making their way into the first cave, they were getting pelted with sleet. The ground quickly became slick and difficult to walk on and the sleet quickly coated their clothing and stung their faces as they made their way into the cave.

"Look at this," said Swifty as they moved saddlebags and packs around in the cave to create a sort of wall at the entrance to help keep the cold and wind out. There in a fissure in the wall was a pile of firewood and a small tin of matches that had been dipped in wax to make them waterproof. Next to the firewood were two battered cans of Dinty Moore's Stew.

"It looks like we found one of old O.J.'s caves."

"We owe O.J. a good bottle of scotch."

"Bottle of scotch my ass. From the looks of this storm we owe him a case of scotch," snorted Swifty.

"You got no argument from me," replied Kit.

They pushed the packs up against the cave opening to cut down on the wind and the sleet and retreated to the back of the cave where Kit dug a shallow fire hole, and they started a small fire.

"As Big Dave taught us, make a small fire and stay close to it and stay warm. Make a big fire and you can't get close to it so you burn on one side and freeze on the other."

"Swifty, some days you surprise me with your wisdom."

"As usual, you're just jealous."

Kit snorted in derision. After a quick hot meal of freeze dried pasta, both men unrolled their sleeping bags and were quickly fast asleep.

CHAPTER NINETEEN

Kit woke up to silence. The storm had passed and it was very cold and dark inside the cave. The small fire was out. Kit slipped out of his sleeping bag which was coated with a light dusting of snow. He listened carefully, but all he could hear was the occasional gust of wind and loud snoring from Swifty's side of the cave. The only thing his nose detected was a smoky smell left over from the camp fire.

Kit crawled to the front of the cave and looked out. It was dark and overcast and everything seemed to be coated with sleet. He crawled over to the packs by the entrance and slipped outside. The storm was over and the wind had died down, but it was still very cold and slippery. He made his way over to the indenture in the stone side of the mountain and all he found were some broken hobbles. The horses were gone. Kit picked up the hobbles and looked around for signs. There were none. He realized the storm must have driven the horses out of the indenture, and they then drifted with the wind.

He returned to the cave and crawled back inside. He started a small fire and pulled out a frying pan and some food from the packs by the entrance to the cave. Kit waited for the fire to take hold and then he proceeded to put the coffee pot over the now burning fire.

When he started cooking bacon in the frying pan, Swifty woke up.

"I must have died and gone to bacon heaven," said Swifty.

"Better that than bacon hell," replied Kit.

"Storm over?"

"Storm is gone and so are the horses."

"The horses are gone?"

"Yep. I figure the wind shifted and forced them out of the rocks, and then they just drifted with the wind. God knows where they are now."

"Well it's a good thing we got our hiking boots on," said Swifty.

"That's my boy, ever the optimist."

"It does present us with a problem," said Swifty as he surveyed the packs they had piled up at the mouth of the cave.

"We can cache most of this here and head back to Dutch Joe's on foot. It might even make us harder to spot."

"What about the diamonds?"

"We bury them in this cave and push the packs to the back of the cave and make sure we erase any sign of us using this place."

"Works for me," said Swifty.

Swifty began going through the packs and filling up two day packs with essentials for their trip back. While Kit dug up the fire pit and buried the diamonds in a hole two feet deep. After filing in the hole Kit then rebuilt the fire on top of the hole hiding the gems.

After a breakfast of bacon and beans and coffee, both men checked their packs and then their weapons and ammunition supply.

"Even though we'll be on foot, we should make good time since we'll be going downhill, and we know where we're going," said Kit.

"I have a thought," said Swifty.

"God we wouldn't want to miss a moment like that," said Kit.

"You're such a wise ass."

"Wise is correct. The other part I'm not so sure of."

"Do you want to hear this or not?"

"Okay, okay, what have you got this time?"

"I think we would be better to keep going east until we get around this part of the mountain and then go down by the east fork of the creek instead of the way we came up to the snow field."

"Why?"

"Because I think they would be waiting for us to come back down the same way we went up. This way we can get down and be behind them without them knowing where we are."

"Actually, that's a very good idea and that's exactly what we're going to do."

By the time they exited the cave and erased all signs of activity around the outside of the cave, the overcast sky had lightened and the sleet covering everything around them had started to melt.

Kit took a GPS reading on the site of the cave and then starting walking to the east. After about half an hour they found a game trail that was headed southeast, and they began to follow it.

After another hour they stopped to rest, and they could hear water running over rocks. Moving toward the sound they found the east fork of the creek that they were looking for.

They walked single file on the west bank of the creek and made their way almost directly south. They made good time and soon passed the split in the creek where they had taken the west fork of the creek on their way up to the snow field.

By now the sky had lightened and the sleet was almost all melted. They had to be careful as the rocks were still slippery, but their hiking boots had good ribbed soles and they managed to get good traction as they walked down stream.

Suddenly, Swifty raised his right hand in a sign to stop. Then he pushed the hand down. Both men stopped and knelt on the creek bank.

Swifty motioned to Kit to stay and then he slipped into the brush and disappeared from sight. He made no sound that Kit could hear and Kit reached up to his shoulder and brought his AR-10 down and checked the safety.

Five minutes later, Swifty was back and he arrived as silently as he had departed.

"I smell a campfire about a quarter mile down the creek. I can't see anything because of all the brush. Let's slip up on it and keep as quiet as possible."

Kit nodded his assent and the two men slowly and carefully made their way through the brush and parallel to the trail they had been following.

The thick brush finally began to thin and they came to the edge of a clearing near the creek. They could see a tent and a smoldering campfire and at least one pack that seemed partially open. There was no sound of any kind.

The wind shifted and Swifty's eyes suddenly widened. "Do you smell that?" he whispered to Kit.

Kit sniffed the stiffening breeze and then he smelled what Swifty had. The wind carried the faint coppery smell of fresh blood.

Kit stayed put while Swifty moved around the outside of the camp so he could check for any other presence. When he found none, he stood up on the other side of the camp and waved to Kit.

Both men cautiously approached the tent. When they were in front of it, Swifty leaned down and pulled the canvas door open. The blood smell was strong. Inside the tent were the two young backpackers. Both of them had their throats slit. The inside of the tent was a pool of blood.

Swifty knelt down and stared inside the tent. He saw nothing out of order except for the bloody bodies. Satisfied, he stood up. "This just happened in the last hour or so."

"Who the hell would do this to these two greenhorns? They were harmless."

"The word were is the correct term to use, Kit. Make sure you don't touch anything. I don't want any cops investigating this crime scene to get the wrong idea about us and these bodies."

Kit just shook his head.

"My guess is this is the work of the same outfit that killed Frosty Stubbs and his bartender and then burned down the mercantile building around them."

"Why kill these two?"

"Somebody wants no competition and these two were just in the way. They were in the wrong place at the wrong time."

"So we should assume they are looking for us."

"Of course they are. Chances are they think we're still up on the snow field and they had to hunker down somewhere during the storm so my guess is they're still up there. We need to keep going."

Kit and Swifty resumed their downstream journey and did so with a slightly faster pace fueled by what they had just witnessed.

Within a short time they came to the next eastern fork that they had previously taken.

They pushed on and about an hour later they stopped to rest. They sat on flat rocks on the edge of the creek. Each of them took a drink of water from their canteens and chewed on a piece of jerky. Suddenly Swifty raised his head. "Did you hear that?" he whispered.

Kit cocked his head and listened. He could hear the distinctive sound of a horse's shoed hooves clattering over rocks. Both of them slipped into the brush and knelt down.

Soon the source of the noise came around a bend of the creek. An older brown mare with a lanky male rider came into view. The man was wearing the distinctive red shirt of a Wyoming Game Warden.

Swifty stepped out of the brush into the open and Kit joined him. The warden seemed surprised to see them and he reined in his horse with caution in his eyes.

"Howdy Warden," said Swifty.

"Howdy. I'm Wyoming Game Warden Merle Anders. Who might you boys be?"

"I'm Swifty Olson and this here is my partner, Kit Andrews. We're from Kemmerer."

"Kemmerer? What are you boys doing up in this country?" asked Anders as he nervously took in the rifles that Kit and Swifty were carrying on their shoulders.

"It's a long and unique story, Mr. Anders, but the fact is we're out looking for an airplane crash site."

"Airplane crash? I ain't heard of no airplanes crashing up here in the Wind River Mountains for a long time."

"You'd be right as this crash happened back in 1928."

Anders looked stunned. "1928!"

"That is correct, sir."

"How the hell would you ever be able to find a plane that crashed in 1928s up in this rugged country?"

"Not an easy task, as I keep telling my partner," said Swifty.

"Maybe I should explain," said Kit. He then proceeded to tell Mr. Anders the story of the ill-fated flight of Wild Bill Hopper.

"That's quite a story, Mr. Andrews."

"Call me Kit, Mr. Anders."

"You say your name is Kit Andrews?"

"Yes sir."

"It seems to me I've heard your name before. Are you familiar with a sheep rancher down in Kemmerer by the name of Big Dave Carlson?"

"Yes sir. Big Dave is my boss. I work for him as a foreman."

"You boys wouldn't mind showing me some identification, would you?"

"Not at all, Mr. Anders," said Kit as he and Swifty produced their driver's licenses and handed them to Mr. Anders.

Anders looked over the licenses and then handed them back.

"You boys are packing some pretty high powered hardware," said the game warden as he nodded toward the rifles both men were carrying.

"They're for protection, Mr. Anders."

"Protection from what?"

"There've been some really bad things happen around us on this trip and we decided to hedge our bets on more powerful protection."

"What kind of things?"

"Well, the Buckskin Crossing Mercantile and Bar was burned to the ground and the owner, Frosty Stubbs and his bartender were murdered. Someone set the fire to try to cover it up."

"Stubbs murdered! When did this happen?"

"It was just a couple of days ago. You can check the story out with the sheriff Wylie Hunt or with Luke Code the foreman of the Wine Glass Ranch."

"I know Sheriff Hunt and I also know Luke."

"There's one more thing, Mr. Anders. We just passed a camp about three miles back upstream where two backpackers, a man and a woman were murdered in their tent."

The game warden's facial expression suddenly hardened. "You found the bodies!"

"That's right. We came on the camp as we hiked downstream. The camp appeared deserted, but we could smell blood. We pulled up the canvas door on the tent, and they were inside. Someone had slit their throats. The tent floor was covered in blood."

"Did either of you touch anything?"

"We didn't touch anything except for the canvas door of the tent. You can ease off the tension, Mr. Anders. You and both of us know that cutting an animal or a human's throat is messy and bloody work. If we were involved, we'd have blood all over our clothes."

The game warden seemed to exhale a sigh of relief.

"I believe you, Kit, but this is going to create a full blown investigation. There hasn't been a killing in this wilderness area in my memory, and I've had this job for seventeen years. Could you boys show me where this camp is?"

"We'd be happy to lead you to the camp," said Kit.

"I'll need to call this in said the game warden. He dismounted and tied his horse off to a nearby bush and then pulled a satellite phone out of his saddle bags.

He stepped away from Kit and Swifty for a short distance, and then made his call where he was out of earshot.

He was only on the phone for a few minutes, and then he returned to where Kit and Swifty were standing.

"I called in the incident and the sheriff will be sending out two deputies right away. They want me to guard the crime scene until they get there. So I'm ready when you boys are."

Kit and Swifty headed upstream with Anders following behind them on horseback. It took them a little over an hour to reach the camp. Anders motioned for the two cowboys to stay with his horse, and he advanced to the tent on foot. By now the tent was thick with flies and after the game warden reached the tent and pulled open the canvas flap, he stepped back and bent over at the waist and vomited on the ground. When he was finished, he returned to his horse and took his canteen from the saddle and washed out his mouth.

"God damn it, that's a terrible scene. I'm sorry about the side show, but my stomach just couldn't handle it."

"No need to be sorry, Mr. Anders, it made us sick too," said Swifty.

Anders recovered enough to pull his GPS out of his shirt pocket and take a reading. After the GPS acquired enough satellites and was active he then wrote down the location information on a small notebook he had in his shirt pocket. He tore the page out of the notebook and handed it to Kit.

"I'll call this in, but if you meet the deputies on your way down the trail, please give them this to help them find this location."

Kit accepted the paper and put it in his shirt pocket. "We'll be glad to help out Mr. Anders. Is there anything else you need us to do?"

"When you get back down, contact the sheriff's office and give them your account of finding the crime scene."

"Will do, Mr. Anders.'

"Thanks, Kit."

"Would you mind a piece of advice, Mr. Anders?"

"What's that?"

"Stay alert. Whoever did this is still on the loose. Don't make yourself their next victim."

"Good advice, Kit. I plan on setting up in those rocks just up the trail where I can see both upstream and downstream. I don't like surprises any more than the next guy."

Kit and Swifty shook hands with the game warden and continued their hike downstream.

After they had hiked back down to where they first met the game warden, they stopped to rest and had a drink of water and a piece of jerky.

"So tell me, Kit. Was the game warden a real game warden or is he another phony keeping track of us?"

"I think he's the real deal. Between the surprise about Frosty Stubbs and the tossing his cookies, either he's a great actor or a real game warden."

"So do we keep on hiking downstream?"

"We keep to the plan which is to hike back to our camp at Dutch Joe's Guard Station and see if anyone's found our horses or get fresh horses."

"I wouldn't be surprised to find our horses standing around our truck and trailer looking for some oats."

"Neither would I, but you never know," said Kit.

They resumed their hike and continued downstream. They made good time as they were walking downhill at a good pace and they were familiar with the trail. They passed the last tributary to the east fork of Squaw Creek where they had discovered the pond and the beaver dam. About half a mile below that tributary Swifty put up his right hand to signal a stop. He went to his knee, and so did Kit.

"What is it?" whispered Kit.

"I'm not sure, but I hear what sounds like someone thrashing around in the willows just downstream from us."

"That doesn't sound like bad dudes unless they're taking a bath."

Swifty grinned. "That's unlikely, unless they are natives of Iceland and like their bath water real cold."

They cautiously slipped off the trail on the west bank of the creek and made their way through the nearby brush. They moved slowly and made as little noise as possible.

"I think I see our bath taker," said Swifty.

"Bath taker?"

"There's a bull moose combining lunch with a bath just to our left in the creek. See him in the middle of those willow trees?"

Sure enough, there was a huge bull moose dining on succulent water plants and pulling them up by the roots. He seemed to be having a great time in the cold creek waters.

"Let's continue downstream in the brush until we are well below him," said Swifty.

"You'll get no argument from me," replied Kit.

After about fifteen minutes Swifty decided they were far enough downstream from the moose to make their way back to the west bank of the creek and continue on the trail.

Back on a familiar path they again regained their stride and began making good time hiking downstream.

They finally reached the small tributary to the west of the creek and had to detour a short distance up the tributary to find an easy place to ford as the creek and the tributary were getting wider and deeper the further downstream they hiked.

Once across the tributary they headed for the junction of the east fork of Squaw Creek with Trail Creek. Almost as soon as they were back on the west bank of the creek, they stopped.

"I smell and hear horse," said Swifty.

"I do as well," said Kit.

They halted on the creek bank and stepped back into the brush and knelt there.

Within minutes they could see three men on horseback with one of them leading a pack horse heading upstream.

"I recognize the first two guys. Those are the two deputies we saw at Buckskin Crossing. They must be responding to the game warden's satellite phone call."

"Who's the third guy?"

"I don't know, but he's wearing a Wyoming Highway Patrol shirt and pants and he's wearing that Smokey the Bear hat they always wear."

Swifty and Kit stepped out of the brush and waved to the three oncoming horsemen.

The three riders reined in their horses and the two deputies were quick to acknowledge Kit and Swifty.

All three men dismounted and Deputy Slater and Deputy Eckert introduced the third man as Bob Murphy, a sergeant in the Wyoming Highway Patrol.

"You boys headed upstream to help out the game warden?" asked Kit.

"That's right," said Slater. "We got a satellite call to help him with what sounded like two homicides. You two know anything about it?"

"We found the bodies. They were still in their sleeping bags and still in their tent," said Kit.

"I have a note for you from Ranger Anders. He asked me to give it to you if I saw you."

"How were they killed?" asked Slater as he took the note from Kit.

"It was real up close and personal. They had their throats cut."

"Oh, God, this is going to be messy. Eckert, did we bring two plastic body bags?"

"Actually I think we have three," said Deputy Eckert.

"Where are your horses, boys?" asked Murphy.

"We got caught in that storm last night and we holed up in a small cave. The horses must have drifted off with the wind. They were gone this morning. You didn't happen to see two saddle horses and a pack horse on your way up here did you?"

"Nope, but we did see some fresh tracks coming downstream. They're probably headed back to your camp or wherever they last had a good bag of oats," said Deputy Slater with a laugh.

"Where are you boys camped?" asked Murphy.

"We have a base camp next to Dutch Joe's Guard Station," answered Swifty.

"We best be going," said Deputy Slater.

"Good luck," said Kit.

"Good luck to you boys as well. You got a long walk ahead of you."

The three men mounted their horses and were quickly out of sight as they rounded a bend in the trail by the creek.

Kit and Swifty got to their feet and resumed their hike downstream. The stream got wider and deeper the father down they hiked and the trail got wider and less rocky.

After a couple of hours they found the junction with Trail Creek and they crossed over Trail Creek where it was shallow and headed west on the south bank of the creek.

After another hour and a half they came within sight of Dutch Boy Guard Station and their truck and trailer.

When they got to their camp, there were their three horses tied off on the horse trailer.

"Deserters, traitors," snarled Swifty to the three uncaring horses.

Kit laughed at his partner's antics and took off his pack and threw himself on the ground.

"Wake me when supper's ready," said Kit.

"You're the cook! How can I have supper ready if the cook is asleep?"

"You're the one always talking about being creative. Think of something creative."

Swifty's response was to stagger back from the truck with two cold beers. He lowered himself to the ground and tossed a beer to Kit.

Neither man spoke while they drank their beer and relaxed their muscles.

"Do we have any more beers in the truck cooler?" asked Kit.

"We have about half a cooler of beers," replied Swifty.

"Maybe we could each drink about six beers and we could call that supper."

"As stupid an idea as that is, it almost makes sense to me," said Swifty.

After about twenty minutes Kit was able to get his body off the ground and reasonably upright. He lurched in the general direction of their packs and soon began the preparation of their supper.

Swifty pulled himself up and fed and watered the horses during which time he continued to berate them for being disloyal beasts.

Kit was almost finished with cooking supper when Nix appeared out of the back door of the Dutch Joe cabin.

"Hey, good to see you guys made it back. I was worried when your horses showed up without any riders. I tied them up to your trailer. I looked them over and I couldn't see anything wrong with them. I hope I did the right thing."

Nix was obviously nervous and Kit tried to put him at ease by telling him that he had done the right thing by catching the horses and tying them up. He asked Nix to join them for supper. Nix eagerly complied.

"How did the horses get loose?" asked Nix.

"The storm hit and we found a small cave, but the horses drifted off with the wind, and when we woke up they were gone.

"So you guys walked all the way down from over 11,000 feet high?"

"Whatever it was, we walked it," said a sullen Swifty.

"Wow, that must have been tough on both of you."

"We fared better than the two backpackers we saw earlier," said Swifty.

"What do you mean? What happened to them?"

"Someone killed them while they were sleeping in their tent last night."

"Killed them!"

"That's what I said."

"Who would do that and why?"

'I have no idea, Nix. I'm just sorry it happened, and that we had to be the ones who found the bodies. It was an ugly sight."

"I can't imagine what it was like. I've never seen anyone who was killed."

"They weren't just killed, they were butchered, Nix."

"They were butchered," said Nix in a shocked voice!

"The killer or killers slit their throats. It was really a bloody scene."

Nix just sat there in shock, unable to speak. His face was white and seemed to be drained of blood.

Kit walked over and patted Nix on the head. "I know it sounds awful, but it really was worse than it even sounds."

"Oh, my God," moaned Nix.

"Here, try this," said Swifty as he handed Nix a cup of coffee with a shot of brandy in it.

Nix sipped at his coffee cup and sat there in stunned silence.

He was still sitting there when Swifty helped Kit clean up the supper dishes and put things away.

When they were done, Swifty poured two cups of coffee for him and Kit and liberally added some brandy."

"I'll have another, if that's okay," said Nix who had suddenly come out of his state of shock.

"You bet," said Swifty as he refilled Nix's cup with coffee and another generous shot of brandy.

"I forgot to ask if you had any luck looking for the crash site," said Nix.

Kit looked at Swifty and Swifty nodded his assent.

"We think we may have found the site, but we're not sure. We found some old wood and it's possible it could have come from an airplane of that era, but we're not sure. Then the storm hit and we had to seek shelter. We wandered around until we found the cave. We waited out the storm in the cave and when the storm was over, we came out and the horses were gone."

"I could see the storm up in the mountains, but we only got some wind down here," said Nix.

"We got a lot more than wind," said Swifty.

"Are you guys going back up to try looking at the same site again?"

"We'll head out first thing in the morning. Want to join us?"

"I wish I could, but my assignment is to remain here at the station unless I get ordered to do something else."

"Tell you what, Nix. If we find something that looks like part of an old airplane, we'll call you on the satellite phone and let you know what we found."

"That would be great," said Nix.

Within half an hour there was no sign of life from the Dutch Joe Guard Camp or from the base camp of Swifty and Kit. Everyone, including the horses, was sound asleep.

* * *

A few miles away a one ton crew cab pickup truck with a long six horse trailer pulled off the road and came to a stop. Five men got out of the truck and began to make a quick camp. Within an hour they had made a quick supper and slipped into warm sleeping bags. They made no effort to remove anything else from the truck or the trailer. In another fifteen minutes they too were all sound asleep.

CHAPTER TWENTY

Kit was up at dawn and had soon whipped up a hearty breakfast of eggs, bacon, and some canned fruit along with his usual brand of strong coffee. As he was finishing up Swifty appeared at the picnic table.

"Did you take care of the horses?"

"I did, not that they deserved it, the disloyal bunch of them," said Swifty.

Almost as if on cue, Nix appeared at the back door of the Dutch Joe Guard Station cabin. Immediately his nose was sniffing the air.

"Is that breakfast I smell?"

"Right again, Mr. Ranger. How do you do it?" said Swifty.

"Well, this time I've got something to add to the meal," said Nix.

"And what might that be?" asked Swifty.

Nix pulled his hand from behind his back and produced a half pint of fresh cream.

"I thought the coffee might go better with some of this."

"You'd be 100% correct, Nix. Kit's coffee needs something to tone it down. His coffee is so strong my spoon can stand straight up in it."

"You don't like my coffee, make your own," snorted Kit.

"Oh I like your coffee, but it could use a little toning down is all," said Swifty with a grin.

The three men sat down and began eating, and the mound of food Kit had prepared quickly disappeared.

Swifty pushed his plate back and poured himself another cup of coffee with a liberal dose of the fresh cream.

"Ahh, that's much better," he said.

Kit ignored him and poured himself another cup and refilled Nix's cup as well.

An hour later, Kit and Swifty had replenished the supplies on the pack horse from stores in their truck and then they were quickly on their way back up stream.

They made good time retracing their steps from the previous two days and were also blessed with good, sunny weather. After stopping for lunch they met Game Warden Anders and the two deputies and the state trooper on the trail. The lawmen had the two bodies of the hikers in body bags lashed on the back of their pack horse.

All of the men dismounted and allowed their horses to drink from the creek while they took swigs from their canteens.

"Did you find anything interesting at the crime scene, Mr. Anders?" asked Kit.

Anders screwed the top back on his canteen and slung it over his saddle horn.

"Not really. I did find some boot prints, but the storm and the melting ice washed out most of the prints. I can't say I found anything very useful."

"That's too bad. I was hoping the killers got a little careless and left some clues behind."

"Storm like that pretty much wipes things clean. It's likely they counted on that and the fact that it could have been weeks before anyone found the bodies."

"You boys headed back up the mountain?" asked Murphy.

"Yep. We're still looking for that old plane wreck site."

"Well, good luck with the search, but it's got to be like looking for a needle in a haystack of needles. Can't be much left after all these years."

"You're right Sergeant. Those old planes were pretty flimsy to begin with and after years of snow, wind, cold and intense sunlight, not much would survive," answered Kit.

The five men shook hands and the two groups continued on their respective journeys.

It was about two o'clock when Kit and Swifty halted for a rest. They watered their horses and sat on rocks for a bite of jerky and a drink of water from their canteens.

"Do you recognize this place?" asked Kit.

Swifty looked around him and shook his head with a negative motion.

"This here is the site of our cache."

Swifty stood and carefully looked around them. "I don't see my cross."

Kit stood and walked over to the large rock between them and the creek. He brushed the snow still on the upper part of the rock and there was Swifty's cross.

"How did you know it was here?" asked Swifty.

"I took a GPS reading and entered this site as a waypoint."

Swifty stepped forward and began to remove the rocks in front of the small cave where he had stored their supplies.

"Don't do that. Leave it as it is. We aren't done here and we might end up needing this cache."

Swifty stopped and began replacing the rocks. When he was done, he and Kit remounted their horses.

"You're right. This thing isn't over, and I got a bad feeling that I can't seem to shake. I think we got more trouble ahead of us."

"I hate to agree with you, but I think you're feeling is correct," answered Kit.

A short time later they were sitting on their horses at the edge of the snow field where they had found Hopper and the diamonds.

"What do we do now?" asked Swifty.

Before Kit could answer, he felt a projectile pass close to his ear at a very high speed. He felt the bullet before he heard the report of the rifle that fired it.

"Get down," he yelled to Swifty as he dove off his saddle to the ground, keeping one of the reins in his hand.

Both men had slipped off their horses and onto the ground. Each of them still held on to their horse by hanging on to one of the reins.

Two more shots rang out, and Kit could hear them ricochet off the rocks just above them. He got to his knees and pulled his rifle from the scabbard and grabbed an ammo box from his saddle bag. He then let go of his horse and rolled behind a pile of rocks that looked to provide some decent cover from the unseen shooters.

Kit removed his cowboy hat and peered out through a crack in the rocks looking for the source of the rifle fire. He saw nothing, and then he looked to his side for Swifty and saw him crouched behind two large rocks that gave him good protection.

The shooting had stopped and Kit could see the horses were about thirty yards away in a small draw created by large boulders.

"Can you see anything?" he asked.

"Nothing," answered Swifty.

Swifty still had his cowboy hat on and as he slowly rose to look over the rocks. His efforts were rewarded with three high powered rifle bullets smacking into the rocks just next to him. He immediately dropped down to the ground and yelled to Kit, "I don't think they like me."

Kit continued to look through the small slit in the rocks and yelled over to Swifty. "Put your hat on a stick and push it up slowly."

Swifty found a stick and slowly pushed his cowboy hat up and to the side of the boulders. The hat drew three more bullets and while they were close, none of them hit the hat.

Kit saw the rifle flashes erupt from a small rise made up of rocks directly to their west. Satisfied that he had the shooters location, he moved to his left and pulled down the bipod on his AR-10 and turned on his EO-Tech holographic sight.

He lay in a prone position and adjusted his rifle until he had a clear field of fire to the shooters position.

Satisfied with his position, Kit waited. Both he and Swifty knew few shooters had much patience, so they waited for the shooters to make a move.

They didn't have long to wait. After about five minutes, Kit could see one of them peer around a small pile of rocks. He had a pair of binoculars and was trying to make sure where his target was.

"Once I start shooting, you move to your right and flank them while I've got their heads down," Kit said in a clear voice to Swifty.

Swifty nodded that he understood and rose to his knees.

Kit waited for another minute as the shooter got more curious and exposed more of his upper body. Kit estimated the range at ninety to one hundred yards and he adjusted his sight accordingly. The EO-Tech holographic sight placed a red dot on exactly where the bullet would arrive.

Taking a deep breath and then letting out half of it, Kit slowly squeezed the trigger of his AR-10. A .308 caliber Match

Grade 178 grain bullet flew to the target and the binoculars and the shooter's head flew backwards and out of sight.

A second head quickly came into view as someone next to the shooter tried to come to the aid of his injured comrade. A second shooter opened fire on Kit's position and the bullet whizzed over Kit's head. The shooter fired a second time and the bullet smashed into the rocks next to Kit.

"That's enough of that shit," thought Kit. Kit fired at the second shooter's position and as fast as he could pull the trigger, he sent five rounds smacking into the rocks around the shooter's position. The AR-10 was a sniper rifle in semi-automatic design and all he had to do was pull the trigger to fire a round instead of having to pull back a bolt and drive another round into the chamber of the deadly rifle. The holographic sight only made the rifle more effective.

Kit waited, but saw no more movement from the small rise. After almost twenty minutes Swifty appeared to the north of the rise and waived his rifle at Kit.

Kit retrieved the horses and when he had them under control, Swifty had made his way back to Kit.

"What did you find?" asked Kit.

"One guy with most of his head missing. There's also a blood trail leading back down the hill. The rest of them had lit out. Nice shooting, by the way."

"Any ID on the dead guy?"

"Nope. Pockets had been pulled inside out."

"How many of them?"

"It looked like there were five so now there's only four and one of them has to be hurt."

"Any weapons?"

"No weapons. They must have taken the dead guy's gun with them. I did find their brass. They were shooting several guns. I found .300 Win Mag, .308, and an 8mm. Based on their rate of fire, it looks like hunting rifles."

"How did they get up here? Did you see any horses?"

"No horses or tracks, but I did hear what sounded like dirt bike motors."

"Dirt bikes in a wilderness area?"

"I don't think they're exactly what you would call law-abiding citizens who really gave a shit about wilderness regulations."

"Why would they want to shoot and kill us when they don't know if we had the diamonds? Shoot us and they'd never get their hands on the stones."

"Maybe they were trying to get us to surrender. They did have surprise on their side and a five to two edge."

"The edge didn't do them much good. They certainly weren't professional shooters," said Kit.

"Thank God for that. They were careless and stupid and at least one of them paid for it," said Swifty.

"What do you think we should do now?" asked Kit.

"We go after the four dumb bastards who tried to fill us with lead. I don't plan to try to sleep with one eye open tonight."

"I have an intense dislike for someone who is trying to kill me, but I think chasing them would be a waste of time. They have a half an hour head start, and they're hightailing it out of here on dirt bikes. Plus I don't want to give them an easy ambush target."

"So, what do you propose we do?"

"I think we entice them to follow us and give us a chance to set up an ambush of our own."

"As much as I would like to chase down those assholes, I concede to the wisdom of your plan. Besides, I like ambushes when we're doing the ambushing. Where do we go?"

"We head back up to the snowfield where we found Mr. Hopper and we act like we are still looking for something."

"Works for me."

Kit handed Swifty the reins to his horse and both men quickly swung into the saddle. With Swifty in the lead they rode over to the last position they had seen the shooters and then Swifty followed their trail for about half a mile.

They soon found where the shooters had stashed their dirt bikes. One lone bike remained and it was easy to see from horseback that the tires had been slit.

"Looks like they wanted to make sure we didn't use the dead shooter's bike," said Swifty.

"I'd rather have a horse anyway," said Kit.

Swifty dismounted and handed his horse's reins to Kit. Then he knelt down in the dirt and studied the marks left in the dirt by the bikes.

"Four bikes by my count. They left and headed southwest. I see a small blood trail by the bikes and then it disappears. You must have nicked one of them with one of your shots."

"It's more likely that I nicked him with a ricochet off those rocks. I put five rounds into his position"

"Either way, one of them is not going to be at full strength and he'll likely slow them down."

"It doesn't' matter. We stick to the plan and head up to the snowfield," said Kit.

Kit held out the reins and Swifty grabbed them and remounted his horse.

"I say let's see where these boys are headed," said Swifty.

"Hell would be an appropriate destination in my humble opinion, but if we don't follow them my guess is they have to come looking for us."

"You're right. I know you're right, I just want another shot at those cowards."

"My guess is that you'll get all the shots you can handle. Anyone willing to commit murder for some diamonds is desperate enough to do anything."

Kit turned his horse's head and led the way back up the mountain. Swifty took one last look in the direction the shooter's had fled and reluctantly turned his horse around to follow Kit.

CHAPTER
TWENTY-ONE

Snake pulled his dirt bike off the trail that ran by the creek and into the cover of a small grove of trees that created a natural screen from anyone looking down from above their positions.

The other three riders followed suit and like Snake, they shut their engines off and dismounted from their dirt bikes.

Digger helped Rocky off his bike. Rocky was bleeding from wounds in his right arm and his right leg. Digger took off Rocky's jacket and shirt and used water from his canteen to wash out the wound. Then he took some sulfa packets from his bike bag and tore one open. He carefully sprinkled the contents of the packet on the wound in Rocky's arm.

"Get your pants off," he ordered.

"Bullshit. I ain't taking my pants off for you or nobody."

"Suit yourself. If you don't want to take the pants off, I'll just cut this leg of your pants off."

"Jesus! Don't cut my pants. Those suckers cost me fifty bucks."

"Look asshole. Your fifty buck pants already got a hole in them and they're getting soaked with blood. You don't want me to fix this wound, just say so. I don't need your grief."

"Okay, okay, I'll take the pants off," said Rocky.

Rocky carefully took off his boots and then his blood-soaked pants. Digger examined the leg wound. He opened another sulfa packet and sprinkled the contents into the wound. He then put clean gauze on the two wounds and taped them in place.

"How is it?" asked Rocky.

"You're one lucky bastard," said Digger.

"The cuts were made by flying chips of rock, not bullets. They're pretty nasty, but they didn't go all the way through like a bullet would have."

Rocky mumbled his thanks and Digger sneered and said, "I'll send you my bill," and stomped off.

"How is he," Snake asked Digger?

"He'll live but he aint' worth much to us as a gun hand. Better to send him back."

Snake nodded and walked back to his dirt bike. He reached into his bike bag and pulled out a satellite phone. He walked through the trees until he was out of earshot of the others and then he turned on the phone and waited for it to acquire a signal.

After a couple of minutes his phone signaled that a connection had been made and Snake proceeded to dial a phone number that he had memorized.

His call reached an answering machine with a message for him to call back when it was more convenient.

Snake sat down on a flat rock and held the satellite phone in his hand and waited.

After about five minutes his satellite phone rang with an incoming call.

Snake answered the phone with "This is Red One."

"Go ahead Red One. Report."

"We attempted to ambush the subjects, but one of our men fired too soon and we ended up in a fire fight."

"What happened to the subjects?"

Snake was a little peeved that the inquiry was about the targets and not about him and his men.

"They were well armed with sniper weapons and they killed Red Four and wounded Red Three. We withdrew, but had to leave Red Four."

"Did Red Four have any ID on his body."

"No. We stripped his body and slit the tires on his dirt bike before we withdrew."

There was silence on the other end of the satellite phone.

Finally the silence was broken. "How badly hurt is Red Three?"

"He has two wounds. One in the leg and one in the arm. He's useless to us as a gun hand."

"Send him back to base and then get back on the trail of the two targets. I want them alive to lead us to the diamonds. Do not hurt them, but it would be helpful if you can find a way to get them to surrender."

"Are you sure they can find the diamonds?"

"They may already have found them. Find a way to use someone or something as a lever to force them to tell you what they've found or force them to find the stones for you."

"Understood. This is Red One out."

There was no answer or acknowledgement from the satellite phone which was now silent.

Snake cursed, stood up, and walked back to his dirt bike where he slipped the phone back into his bike bag.

*   *   *

Kit and Swifty were walking their horses as they approached the snow field where Hopper's airplane had crash landed.

They tied up their horses and put on their snow shoes and proceeded to walk the field in almost the same grid they had walked previously. This time they began from the opposite end of the snow field and in effect were walking the same pattern from the reverse direction.

They found some more artifacts of wood and metal and they laid the artifacts on the edge of the snow field in a side by side pattern.

They left the site of the body of Mr. Hopper alone.

After about two hours, Swifty slipped closer to Kit and whispered, "We've got company."

Kit overcame his natural desire to look up and see what Swifty had noticed, knowing that doing so would announce to their watchers that they had been discovered.

Fifteen minutes later Swifty found another piece of wood from the airplane, and they both walked to the side of the snow field to deposit it next to their growing line of artifacts.

As they turned to return to the snow field and their grid walk, a loud voice rang out.

"Freeze where you are and put your hands up in the air, or we'll shoot you."

Both Kit and Swifty came to a stop and both men raised their hands in the air and turned to face the speaker.

Pretty soon three armed men appeared from the rocks behind where they had been storing their artifacts. All of them were dressed in camouflage pants and shirts as well as baseball hats. All three of them were pointing pistols at Kit and Swifty.

As the three gunmen approached, Kit could see that the larger of the men appeared to be the leader. The other two men were younger and shorter and following the leader by a respectful pace or two.

The gunmen came to within twenty feet of Kit and Swifty and stopped.

"Throw down any weapons you have on you and be quick about it," snarled the leader.

Kit and Swifty slowly reached under their coats and pulled out their pistols from their holsters and gently tossed them down on the soft snow in front of them.

"Get their weapons," said the leader to one of the shorter men.

The short gunman came forward warily and he quickly picked up both Kit and Swifty's pistols. He stepped back a few feet, examined the pistols, and then put them in his pockets and returned to his position next to, but slightly behind the one who appeared to be the leader.

Kit examined the three men. They were all white. The leader was the oldest. He looked to be in his middle forties, and he was dark skinned with brown curly hair and a lot of noticeable tattoos on his face and neck.

The other two men were younger and looked to be in the mid-twenties. They also sported tattoos on their face and neck.

The leader carried his pistol as though he knew what he was doing. The two younger ones were more careless in how they handled their weapons.

"What is it we can do for you boys?" asked Kit.

"You can shut your mouth. I'll do the talking, and you only talk when I want an answer. You understand?"

Both Kit and Swifty nodded their heads that they understood.

"Good. I'm pleased that we understand each other. I see you've been collecting what looks like some kind of junk. Just what is all of this stuff I see lying by the side of this snow field?"

Kit raised his right hand a little higher.

"Okay, you, the tall one. Tell me what you and your partner are doing up here?"

"We're looking for the remains of a U.S. Air Mail pilot named William Hopper, who crash landed here in 1928."

The leader did not look in the least bit surprised and Kit knew he probably wasn't.

"Why in the hell would you be looking for a plane wreck up here that happened in 1928?"

"We were asked by some descendants of Mr. Hopper to try to find his remains up here. An artifact from the plane was found in this area by a cowboy. We've been searching for the crash site and then hopefully for his remains."

"So you have been doing all this hard work just out of the goodness of your heart and with no reward in mind, but finding what's left of some old coot. That seems a little extreme even for a good hearted Christian."

Kit did not respond and just stared at the leader.

"So, Mr. Good Guy, just what have you found here?" said the leader as he pointed at the remnants of the airplane lined up side by side on the edge of the snow field.

Kit did not replay and just stood in place staring at the leader.

"By the way you can address me as Red One. My two assistants are Red Two and Red Five."

"What happened to Red Three and Red Four?" asked Swifty.

Red One stepped forward quickly and in one motion he swung his pistol in a downward arc and hit Swifty on the side of the head, knocking him down to his knees and opening a cut on the side of his face that began to bleed freely.

"I said only speak when I asked you a question, asshole."

He turned to look at Kit with rage I his eyes. "You have trouble understanding my directions, Pal?"

Kit shook his head slowly from side to side.

"I was going to ask which one of you was the sharpshooter, but I'm pretty sure you are," he said. "What's your name, tall guy?"

"My name is Carson Andrews, but my friends call me Kit."

"Well I ain't your friend, Mr. Andrews and I ain't likely to become one anytime soon. Did you shoot my two friends?"

"They were shooting at me. I shot back."

"That don't make me any happier about it Andrews. You and your pal here are going to help us out or neither of you will live to walk off this snow field. Do you understand me?"

By now Swifty had regained his feet and he stood silently with his hands raised, his face still bleeding with the bright red blood spotting the clean white snow at his feet.

"I'll ask again. What is all this junk you have lined up on the snow?"

"These are parts of the U.S. Air Mail airplane that crashed on this snow field in 1928."

"Did you find any other parts that are not lined up on the dirt?"

"We did find the engine. It's about thirty yards to the east of where I'm standing. It's too large and heavy for us to move."

"How about the old coot who was the pilot. Did you find him?"

Kit looked Red One directly in the eyes and said, "No we didn't find him yet. That's why we were still searching this site."

Red One rubbed his unshaved cheek with the sight of his pistol as he stared at Kit and seemed to be thinking over what Kit had told him.

"You didn't find anything else here that you don't have lined up over there?" he said as he pointed at the line of artifacts on the side of the snow field.

"Everything we found is over there," said Kit.

"Well then, it appears to me that you and your buddy need to keep on looking. Me and my boys would love to help you, but we got no snow shoes so we'll just sit on them rocks over there and cheer the two of you on."

Red One motioned to his two gunmen to retreat back to the edge of the snow field, and he began to slowly back away from it and Swifty. He never took his eyes off them and he kept his gun pointed at them.

"Get back to searching and don't get any funny ideas or you'll wind up buried up here with that old coot, Hopper."

Red One and the two others retreated to the edge of the snow field. Kit noticed that they had a great deal of difficulty with their footing in the soft and slippery snow.

Kit and Swifty walked back to their last search point and slowly began to continue their grid search.

"What's the plan?" whispered Swifty.

"I've got an idea. I'll let you know when I'm ready," answered Kit softly.

The two men continued their grid search. After almost an hour they had walked over the spot where they had reburied Mr. Hopper and they kept on walking.

Twice they stopped and retrieved a piece of wood one time and part of some kind of dial from the instrument panel of the airplane. With each discovery, Kit walked the artifact over to the side of the snow field and laid it down next to the rest of the artifact laid out in a line. He then returned to his last position on the search grid.

By now almost an hour and a half has passed and they were on the far south side of the snow field and about two thirds of the way to the east end.

"Do we have a plan yet?" whispered Swifty.

"We do," whispered Kit.

"In another ten yards, I'll say now and we start running to the east where we found the cave."

"Running? Are you nuts? They'll run us down and shoot us. That's no plan," whispered Swifty.

"No, they won't. Only an expert with a pistol can hit anything at thirty feet and we're a good two hundred feet away from them. Plus they don't have snow shoes and they have to cross the snow field to chase us."

"So we hide in the cave?"

"Nope. There's too much of a chance we could get discovered and cornered. We run up into the rocks and move around the north side of the mountain. Then we head back down the mountain on the east side and get back to our cache. Then we'll see who's on first."

"So my partner is truly nuts, but I must be too, because his goofy idea actually makes sense to me."

"Glad you came over from the dark side."

Kit stole a look over to the north side of the snow field and only Red One was actually keeping an eye on them. The other two were lying back against some rocks like they were sunning themselves at the beach. Kit was pretty sure the three gunmen would first try to cross the snow field to chase them and then turn back to get their dirt bikes. Dirt bikes wouldn't do them much good in the rugged and rocky area south of the snow field. That would put the gunmen on foot and level the playing field for Kit and Swifty.

Kit stared hard at the spot he had picked out in the snowfield and when he and Swifty reached it, he yelled, "Now!"

Both of them ran in their snow shoes to the edge of the snow field and then quickly took off their snow shoes and began running into the higher rocky area to the south.

The gunmen were caught off guard and just as Kit had suspected they immediately followed their instincts and ran onto the snow field. All three of them had trouble keeping their footing and one of them slipped and plunged head first into the snow.

Shots rang out, but at that range no bullets came near Kit or Swifty. Kit and Swifty kept running into the rocks. Kit let Swifty take the lead as he had the best instincts when it came to tracking and moving quickly without being seen or heard.

At one point Kit stole a look over his shoulder from behind a large boulder and he could see that the gunmen were headed for their dirt bikes. He turned and kept running, staying as close to Swifty as he could. They ran at a pace that Swifty set and after fifteen minutes Swifty slowed to a walk.

"Why are we stopping?" said Kit.

"We're not stopping. We're walking and that's part of the pace. We run for fifteen minutes and walk for five. At this pace we'll outrun them and be able to keep going for several hours."

Kit nodded his approval and took in large gulps of fresh air to his aching lungs.

After four sets of Swifty's pace, they found themselves on the east side of the mountain and began moving down. They were careful to move as quickly and quietly as they could, and they stayed in the rocky and more difficult terrain which provided them with lots of cover.

Swifty put up his hand for them to halt and motioned for Kit to get down on the ground. Swifty then moved ahead and quickly disappeared from Kit's view. In five minutes he was back, almost as soundlessly as he had disappeared.

"I can't see them, but I can hear them. They seem to be having a little difficulty moving their dirt bikes through this terrain and their swearing is louder than the engine noise from their dirt bikes."

Kit forced a grin and Swifty returned it.

Swifty found a small dry wash that was probably active in the spring run-off, and they crawled down it for several hundred feet. The wash was like a natural trench and by crawling, nothing of either man was visible above the ground.

When the wash ended, Swifty led them in a route that angled to the north as they descended the mountain. Kit understood that they were staying as far away from the creek and the easier ground around it to make it harder to see or to find them.

After another hour of slipping from rock formation to rock formation as they made their careful descent, Swifty again put up his hand for a halt.

He slid next to Kit and whispered to him. "I think we're very close to the cache. Keep looking up for the cross I scratched on the rock. It should be to our right."

Silently they slowly moved in a gradual descent. Kit was trying to creep forward and look up at the same time. All of a sudden he felt Swifty grab him by the arm. Kit stopped moving and looked up. There was the faint outline of the cross that Swifty had etched into the soft rock above the small cave.

Kit and Swifty waited for a few minutes, testing the wind for smells or sounds and carefully viewing their surroundings. Satisfied that they were alone, the two men crept forward and began to remove the rocks from the front of the small cave. They carefully handled each rock and set them aside as quietly as possible.

Finally they found the tarp that covered their cache. They quickly retrieved the pistols and ammo and checked the pistols to make sure they were still in working condition and loaded. Kit pulled out the first aid kit and survival blankets and the plastic bag of jerky from the cache. He opened the first aid kit and after getting some water from the nearby creek, he cleaned the wound on Swifty's cheek and swabbed it with disinfectant. A small bandage completed his work.

Both men drank creek water and chewed on pieces of jerky.

"Best meal I've had in months," said Swifty.

"Hard to argue with that," replied Kit.

Swifty touched the bandage on his face and looked directly at Kit.

"All in good time Swifty. We need a plan to take care of those three. Plus we don't know how many more of them there are."

"I don't give a rat's ass how many there are as long as I get to repay the big asshole."

"Let's worry more about coming out on top rather than getting personal revenge," said Kit.

"You do it your way, and I'll do it my way," replied a grim Swifty.

CHAPTER TWENTY-TWO

Snake was growing more frustrated by the minute. They lost the two cowboys' trail in the rocky ground, and as Kit had predicted, they found the rugged terrain unsuitable for their dirt bikes and had to dismount and walk their bikes through the rocks.

He finally decided that trying to track and find the cowboys in the rugged terrain was hopeless, and he ordered Red Two and Red Five to follow him as he backtracked until he could find a path that led down to the creek and the level ground next to it.

Once they reached the creek, they took a break and broke out their water bottles. Snake considered using the satellite phone to report in what had happened and then decided the incident was not over and he wasn't done with the two cowboys, especially the tall one who he was sure had engineered the escape. Snake could not believe how they had suckered him. He thought he had them cowed, but he had misjudged them. They were two tough dudes and he would not underestimate them again.

Snake slid the satellite phone back into the saddlebag on his dirt bike. He would call in when he had something good to report. That time was not now.

*   *   *

"What's the plan this time?" asked Swifty.

"My guess is they'll get tired of trying to get through the rocks, and they'll move back to the path by the creek. They probably figure we're trying to get down the mountain, and they'll try to get down first and set up an ambush."

"So what do we do?"

"You're faster at moving in cover, so I need you to move down the mountain to the place where the two branches of the creek meet. I'll be right behind you, but I'll be carrying the food, first aid kit, blankets and the spare ammo. You set up the ambush point and backtrack to me so we can get it set up before they arrive at the ambush point."

"I'm on my way," said Swifty and he quickly slipped into the nearby brush and was gone.

Kit gathered up the supplies they had retrieved from the cache and began to carefully make his way in a controlled descent. He was careful to remain quiet. He didn't want to alert the gunmen that he was around.

After about twenty minutes, his descent was interrupted by the sight of Swifty kneeling on the ground next to a large sagebrush just below Kit.

Swifty put his finger to his mouth as if to warn Kit to remain silent. Kit acknowledged Swifty's signal by touching his finger to the brim of his cowboy hat.

Kit slowly and quietly made his way down to where Swifty was kneeling in the dirt.

"They're about ten minutes away," said Swifty. "Just below me is a spot where the trail is narrow against the creek because of a large pile of boulders. You get up on top of the rock pile, and I'll be behind a large rock on the other side of the creek. When the last one of them is in the narrow spot, I'll challenge them to throw down their weapons. If they don't, we shoot them. Understand."

"I got it," said Kit.

Swifty reached out and put his hand on Kit's arm. "Kit, if they don't throw down, don't hesitate and shoot to kill."

Kit nodded his agreement and Swifty removed his hand from Kit's arm and slipped into the rocks.

Kit carefully made his way down to the edge of the rock pile Swifty had pointed out to him. When he reached the rock pile, he looked up to check on where Swifty was, but he was unable to see him from where he knelt. After making sure that his pistol was secure, Kit began to climb up the rock pile.

Kit had no sooner climbed up to the top of the rock pile than he heard voices coming from upstream. He had a good vantage point, and he could clearly see Swifty crouching behind a large boulder on the other side of the creek.

The ambush point was far enough down the mountain that the creek was only three feet wide, but was full of rushing water resulting from the run-off of melting snow high above them.

Kit lay flat on the top of the rocks and tried to slow his breathing as the voices from upstream got louder as the gunmen approached the ambush site.

Finally the gunmen appeared. All three of them were walking their dirt bikes in a single file formation. They did not seem any too happy about their current situation. One of the shorter gunmen was making the most noise.

"When we find them two drug store cowboys I say we hang them upside down over a nice hot fire and watch their brains boil out through their ears."

He was about to add more comments in a similar vein when a loud voice rang out.

"Hold it right there. Drop your weapons or we'll shoot you right where you stand."

"Bullshit!" said Snake. "Unless you're planning on throwing rocks at us you guys ain't got no guns."

Swifty fired one round and a hole appeared in the gas tank of the dirt bike Snake was holding onto.

"The next round will be between your eyes, Dirt Bag. Drop your weapons now!"

Snake looked up, and he saw Kit on top of the rock pile with his pistol pointed directly at Snake. The look on Kit's face told Snake this was no bluff.

"Shit!" said Snake. "They got guns and they got us dead to rights. Drop your weapons, Boys."

Snake and Red Two reached out and dropped their pistols in front of them and put their hands up in the air.

Red Five acted like he was going to drop his pistol, but then quickly brought it up to fire at Swifty. Kit shot him between the eyes. Red Four's fingers twitched as though he was trying to gain control of his weapon and then dropped to the ground like a sack of potatoes, his gun still in his hand and a surprised look on his face.

"Cover them, Kit," said Swifty.

Kit rose to his knees and kept his pistol pointed directly at Snake and Red Two.

Swifty came out from behind the large boulder, and he splashed across the shallow stream. He picked up the gunmen's weapons from the ground, including the one still in the hand of the dead gunman and then he ordered the two men to lie on the ground on their bellies and keep their hands behind their heads.

Swifty quickly searched both gunmen and relieved them of two more guns and three knives. He also found two pairs of handcuffs and used them to handcuff the gunmen's hands behind them.

"Okay Kit, come on down."

Kit climbed down from the rock pile and kept the gunmen covered while Swifty searched the saddlebags on their dirt bikes. He found five scoped hunting rifles and quite a bit of ammunition. He removed the bolts from the rifles and tossed them into the creek. He also found a satellite phone and slipped that into his pants pocket.

Finding nothing else useful in the saddlebags, Swifty turned to face his prisoners. He ordered them to get up in a sitting position and began talking to them, using the barrel of his pistol as a pointer to emphasize what he had to say.

"Here's the deal. We're taking you two down to the ranger station and turning you over to the sheriff. You give us any trouble of any kind on the trip down this mountain and you'll be staying here for eternity. I hope you two buzzards do try something and give me a good excuse to shoot you down like the dogs you are. Are we clear on the rules?"

Both gunmen nodded their heads they understood only too well how serious Swifty was.

Swifty found a short length of rope and tied one end to Snake's handcuffs and the other end to Red Two's handcuffs.

"Try to get away and you will surely trip over each other," said Swifty with a grin.

"Before we start our little journey we'd like a few questions answered and believe me not cooperating will be very painful."

Both of the gunmen stared at Swifty warily.

"What do you want to know?" asked a worried looking Snake.

"Who are you guys working for?"

Swifty's question was met with silence.

"So you two don't feel like you're in a sharing mood?"

Again the two gunmen remained silent.

"Perhaps you both have a hearing problem. At no time am I going to repeat a question after this one time. Who do you work for?"

Both gunmen looked down at the ground and remained silent.

Quick as a flash Swifty drew his pistol and fired it at Snake from a distance of no more than six feet. The bullet found its intended mark and the lower part of Snake's left ear was gone and blood began to gush out of what was left.

Snake screamed out in agony and pain and tried to reach his damaged ear with his handcuffed hands. Red Two's face became drained of all color.

Swifty waited for the screaming to lessen and when it did, he jerked Snake's bleeding head up by his hair.

"Apparently you two dumb shits don't get it. We ain't cops. We're cowboys who are really pissed with all the shit and trouble you two have caused us. If we take you down the mountain and hand you off to the sheriff we get stuck with making statements, appearing as witnesses, and all kinds of other crap that we're not interested in. On the other hand, we can just shoot you two assholes and leave your bodies up here. In five days after all the critters and varmints are done with you, there will be nothing left for anyone to find with the possible exception of some hair and a few bones. All we have to say to the cops is you tried to assault us and we defended ourselves."

Swifty paused to look the two thugs in the eyes.

"Just who do you think they'll be inclined to believe? They'll get to choose between two honest cowboys or you two thieving assholes. Trust me. Society will be better off without either of you."

Swifty released his grip on Snake's hair, turned around and sat down on a nearby rock, keeping his gun pointed at the two captives.

"So, Gents, which will it be? Give us a little information or suffer a painful death? You choose."

"I'll talk, I'll talk," said a trembling Red Two. Snake kept moaning and seemed to be in too much pain to respond to Swifty's demand.

"Much better," said Swifty

Swifty turned slightly to directly face Red Two, and kept his pistol pointed directly at him.

"Who are you working for?"

"Snake here is our team leader. We each have a designation. This is the Red team so Snake is Red One, I'm Red Two and so on. We don't know each other and I don't know anyone's real names. Some of the guys had nicknames like Snake, but we were only allowed to call each other by our Red team designation."

"So, who hired you?"

"I responded to a message in a blog site on the internet. It's where I get most of my jobs."

"Have you ever heard or seen anyone else Snake took orders from?"

"No. When I answered the message on the blog, I got directed to a motel in Rock Springs where a reservation had been made in my name. After I checked into my room, there was a knock on the door and that's how I met Snake."

"Did Snake ever communicate with anyone else outside of the Red Team that you know of?"

"Yeah, he did. He had a satellite phone that he used to report to someone. He would always try to get out of earshot of the rest of us when he made a call, but one of the guys overhead some of what he said and it sounded like he was reporting in to someone. I have no idea who."

Swifty turned to look at Kit.

After the shooting of Snake's ear and during Swifty's rant to the gunmen, Kit had sat silently and made no move to interfere with Swifty.

"Do you have any questions for this bozo?"

"No. He obviously doesn't know much and whoever is running this show has done a lot of work to compartmentalize what they're doing so nobody would know much except their small piece of the deal."

"Do you have your GPS with you, Kit?"

Kit realized Swifty was trying to make sure they kept the GPS with the locations of the dead Mr. Hopper and the location of the diamonds a secure secret.

"It's in the saddlebag on my horse."

"Which we had to leave back at the snow field. Shit!"

"What about the satellite phone," asked Swifty?

"It's in the same place as the GPS, but I think the battery is probably dead by now. I forgot to charge it the last time we were at the ranger station. Plus our rifles are with the same horses."

"Isn't it great that we live in a world of technology," said Swifty with a grin as his fished Snake's satellite phone out of his pants pocket. "Look what I found in Red One's dirt bike saddlebag."

Swifty pushed the power button to turn it on.

"Shit, the battery on this thing is stone dead."

"Hey, at least the pistols work fine," replied Kit with a grin of his own.

"Those damn horses have managed to become a giant pain in my ass on this expedition. They move around more without us than a traveling salesman."

"At least the horses don't need batteries," said Kit with a smile.

Swifty grimaced back at Kit.

"So, do we backtrack and try to find the horses or do we continue our walk down the mountain with Huey and Dewey as our guests?" asked Kit.

Swifty paused for a minute and looked back the way they had come towards the snow field and then back down the mountain where they had been headed.

"I think our best bet is to head down and get rid of these two. The longer we keep them around, the more likely I am to become overcome with a blinding desire to shoot their asses off."

Swifty walked over to where Kit was standing and took him by the arm and pulled him out of earshot of their prisoners.

"If they try anything at all including an attempt to escape, I'm shooting both of them in the head. I meant what I said about us versus them when dealing with the law."

"You might encourage their good behavior by telling them that we don't plan on wounding them because we don't plan on carrying them so they understand exactly what their options are."

"It's a deal."

Swifty used a rag from the saddle bags of the dirt bikes dipped in creek water to clean up Snake's ear. Snake gritted his teeth and said nothing.

Kit walked over to the two dirt bikes and pulled out his knife and slit all four tires.

"You ready, Swifty?"

"I was born ready. Let's move out."

Their progress was slow. This was due to a combination of the rugged terrain and the difficulty their handcuffed and tethered prisoners were having making their way clumsily downstream on the path.

The sun had come out from under the cloud cover, and it actually began to feel hot to the four hikers. There was little shade so after about two hours, Swifty held up his hand for a halt.

"Let's take a water break," said Swifty and the two prisoners walked over to the creek and immediately went down to their knees and leaned down to the creek to drink directly from it. When they were done, they walked over to the shaded rocks that Kit and Swifty were seated on under three large pine trees. The two outlaws sprawled on the ground grateful for the shade.

"Hey you," said Swifty as he poked at Snake with the tip of his hiking boot.

"What are you gonna do, shoot me again?" snarled Snake.

"Watch your mouth Asshole, or I'll give you matching ears," said Swifty coldly.

"What do you want?" answered Snake.

"You're Red One, correct?"

"Yes."

"That was your satellite phone I found, correct?"

"Yes."

"Who were you calling with it?"

"I called a pre-programmed number. I don't know who was on the other end of the call."

"Why did you make the calls then?"

"My instructions were to call in daily with a report."

"A report of what?"

"A report of what you two were doing, where you were, and whether or not you'd discovered the crash site."

"When you found us at the crash site, did you call to report that?"

Snake looked down at the ground and hesitated. Finally he spoke. "No, I was waiting until you found something valuable. I knew my battery was getting low."

"So your boss or whoever is on the other end of your calls hasn't heard from you since when?"

"I called and reported after our failed ambush."

"Did you get new instructions then?"

"My instructions were the same as before, observe and report if you two found something significant."

"You didn't think the crash site was significant?"

"I had the crash site and the two of you. I figured that I'd let you two search the area and find what was to be found and then report it."

"That didn't work out too well, did it?"

"You were lucky, and I was careless."

"Now you're the lucky one, Pal."

'How do you figure? I get my ear shot off and I'm in handcuffs. How is that lucky?"

"I only shot your earlobe off, Crybaby. You're lucky you're a prisoner and not lying dead back up on the mountain with your friends."

"They're not my friends. They were just work associates. I don't' even know their real names."

"So how were you recruited to this little adventure in the Wind River Mountains?"

"Same way as Red Two was. It was all internet and phone calls."

"You wouldn't happen to know anything about two hikers getting murdered. A young man and a young woman had their throats slit in their tent not far from here."

Snake looked up in surprise. "I don't know nothing about no hikers. We didn't murder nobody. The only people I shot at was you two."

"I feel so much better knowing that it was only us that you were trying to kill," said Swifty.

"I wasn't trying to kill you, just control you. I needed you two to find the crash site for us."

"What do you think Kit?" Swifty asked his partner.

"I think he's telling us the truth, or at least whatever semblance of the truth that someone like him understands."

"This is getting confusing," said Swifty.

"We know that at least one treasure hunting group used the women to try to recruit us."

"Correct," said Kit.

"We know the two dead hikers were trying to keep an eye on us so they were working for either the same treasure hunting company or another one."

"Correct again."

"We know these two guys are working for what appears to be a much more aggressive treasure hunting outfit, and one that operates outside the law."

"I agree."

"So who killed the hikers if it wasn't this group of Red guys?"

"Maybe the bad guy company has more than one unit in the field. Someone is controlling this Red unit. Who is to say that they might be controlling other units in the field not only working independent of each other, but ignorant of the existence of any other group," said Kit.

"Then there's the kind of odd lady forest ranger. I think Pat was her name."

"She did seem out of place and too neat to be coming out of the field."

"So who is she working for?"

"I don't know, Swifty, but I do know this. We came up here to find a crash site and try to locate and retrieve the remains of a pretty brave pilot for his family. In addition, we became aware of a valuable cargo that Hopper was carrying in his air mail packet."

"Our personal mission was to find the remains of Hopper and maybe find the valuable cargo and report it to the authorities and let the chips fall where they may."

"I agree," said Swifty.

"And I think we've accomplished what we set out to do with the exception of reporting what we found to the authorities and waiting on the falling chips."

"I'm not very fond of having chips fall on my head," said Swifty. "It's never worked out very well for me."

"The sooner we get down the mountain, turn these two dirt bags over to the sheriff, and inform him of what we found and where it's located, the better."

"I totally agree," replied Swifty.

"Once we're done, we're of no interest to any of these treasure hunting companies no matter how many companies or how many people they have located up in these mountains around us."

"I'd drink to that if we had something to drink," said Swifty.

*   *   *

It took them another three and a half hours, but they finally arrived at the place where Line Creek joined into Squaw Creek and they turned to the west to finish their journey.

They rested and took a water break before they set out on the last leg of their long hike. The two prisoners were quiet and sullen. The fight had long gone out of them. Snake and Red Two had figured out that the team of Swifty and Kit were more than a match for them and any resistance on their part would be painful and dangerous to their health.

The trip back to Dutch Joes Guard Station was slow and painful for Kit and Swifty as well as their prisoners. All of their physical efforts of the day had pushed the two cowboys to the edge of their physical capabilities and the mental and emotional stress was a load unwanted by either of them.

As they came up the trail from the creek to the clearing surrounding the Dutch Joe Guard Station, they were greeted by the sight of their truck and trailer looking intact and unharmed. There was no sign of their horses.

Swifty led the prisoners to the horse trailer, and he removed their handcuffs, only to then handcuff one hand of each of them to the other and then to handcuff the chain of the first handcuff to the frame of the horse trailer.

"There, that ought to hold you," said Swifty.

Snake and Red One promptly dropped to the ground and laid there in an awkward sprawl. Kit then arrived with cups of cold water from the station's water pump and handed them to the two outlaws.

"Why don't you rustle us up something to eat, and I'll go in and find Nix and get him to call the Sheriff on his satellite phone," said Swifty.

"Sounds like a plan to me," said Kit and he turned to the packs in the truck and trailer to find the makings of a meal.

Swifty took a long drink of cold water from the station water pump and then headed for the front door of the ranger cabin.

Swifty had no sooner stepped up on the front porch of the cabin when the front door opened and he was met with a surprise.

"Put your hands in the air, Cowboy, and don't try anything or yell out or it will be the last thing you ever do."

The speaker was a large bald man with a tough looking face that featured the stubble of a beard that looked like it was stronger than any razor. He was wearing what appeared to be ill fitting outdoor shirt and pants that were still stiff and creased. The clothes looked like they had just been taken off the shelf at an outdoor sporting goods store. His shoes were brightly colored tennis shoes.

His eyes were black and seemed devoid of any light. In his hand was a very large pistol and it was pointed directly at Swifty's heart.

Swifty complied, and the man motioned with his pistol for Swifty to enter the cabin. As he stepped inside the front room a second, shorter and smaller man who was dressed like the big one, stepped forward and expertly frisked Swifty. He extracted the pistol in Swifty's belt and an extra ammo magazine from his left front pocket. Satisfied that Swifty was disarmed, the short man motioned for Swifty to be seated in a nearby hardback wooden chair.

"Who are you guys?" asked Swifty.

"We'll do the talking unless we ask you a question and then you better give us a good answer because your life will depend on it. I kid you not."

The short man stepped in front of Swifty and looked him in the eye.

"I'm Mr. Kellogg and this is my associate Mr. James. We believe you have something or have knowledge of where something is located that has great value to us. Do you understand?"

"Yes," said Swifty.

"Excellent. We are off to a good start. Exactly how many of you are there Mr. Cowboy?"

"Just me and my partner."

"Is there anyone else out there?"

"Two prisoners we captured up on the mountain."

"Only two?"

"There were five, but these two are the only ones left."

"I'm impressed. Two cowboys took out three of the Red Team, Mr. James. Are you impressed as well?"

Mr. James looked down at the unarmed and seated Swifty and spat on him.

"The Red Team was a bunch of alley rats and losers that came for the money. I don't see taking them out as much of a big deal."

Swifty slowly turned his face and used his hand to wipe Mr. James spittle off his face.

"What do we do about his partner? He's out by the truck and trailer."

"We wait, Mr. James. His partner will get curious about this one and come looking for him. We'll get the drop on him the same way we did this one."

James went into another room and reappeared with a short length of rope. He pushed Swifty forward on his chair and then tied his hands behind him. James checked his knot and satisfied, he shoved Swifty back onto the chair.

"What now?" asked James.

"We wait," replied Kellogg.

Kit had put together some sandwiches and gave each prisoner a sandwich and a can of pop. He bit into a sandwich and took a sip of pop and looked out toward the ranger cabin.

As Kit chewed on his sandwich, he started having some troubling thoughts. "Something isn't right," he thought. "Swifty hasn't come back, and he's just as hungry as I am. Also, where is Nix? He is always at the cabin, and he always came out to greet us each time we returned to our base camp."

Kit walked over to the cab of the truck and looked under the back seat. There he found his back-up Kimber .45 ACP.

He checked to make sure it was loaded and added two more magazines of ammo to his pockets.

Instead of heading to the front door of the cabin, he walked over to the water pump that was located at the rear of the cabin. He pretended to draw water to a nearby bucket. All the time he kept looking over the ranger cabin. He could see no movement. That was not a good sign.

CHAPTER
TWENTY-THREE

Kit stood still and tried to check his surroundings. He could hear nothing but the wind in the nearby grove of Aspen. He sniffed at air but could smell nothing but the usual scents of a camp. He carefully scanned his surroundings, and he could see nothing that looked out of place.

As he carefully looked around, he took note of a small wooden shed located behind the cabin and slightly to the north. Stacked next to the shed were several cords of split firewood.

He was trying to decide what to do next when fate stepped in. His hearing picked up some foreign noise and as he turned in the direction of the noise, he could see a dust trail rising from the dirt road coming from the north.

The source of the dust trail was a white SUV that soon appeared in the distance and slowed down as it approached the ranger station.

As luck would have it, the SUV slowed to a stop and then pulled to the front of the ranger station.

Kit used this distraction to slip silently closer to the cabin and soon was pressed tightly against the south facing log wall.

Kit was able to peer around the edge of the cabin and he saw that the SUV contained two people, a driver and a passenger in the front seat. The passenger got out on his side of the SUV and started to walk up to the cabin, while the driver just opened his door as though to let more air in the vehicle. Both of them were young men dressed in biking gear. Kit noticed that they had two mountain bikes mounted on a bike rack attached to the back of the SUV.

Before Kit could react, a short, stocky man dressed up like an ad for L.L. Bean came out of the front of the cabin. He could hear the man talking to the two young men, but he could not make out clearly what they were saying.

Whatever the short man had said, the two young men were quickly back in their SUV and headed on their way to the south with a small dust cloud trailing behind them.

Kit was sure that Swifty had walked into a trap, and he was also pretty sure that there was more than one gunman in the cabin.

He was pretty sure they were waiting for him to come looking for Swifty and fall into the same trap.

Kit carefully and quietly retreated back to his previous position behind the cabin. He noted that back door to the cabin was just inside a small covered porch, and he carefully made his way over to the porch. He reached a window next to the porch and he carefully took a look inside. He was looking at a kitchen and it appeared to be empty.

Instead of taking the steps which he feared were likely to make noise, He grabbed a supporting post at the edge of the porch and after placing his foot on the top of the porch he quickly and quietly pulled himself up to the porch level.

The back door was steel and had no window. Kit tried the door knob and it was not locked. He slowly turned the knob with his left hand while he held his pistol in his right hand. He kept his body at a ninety degree angle to the back of the cabin.

The knob was turned as far as it would go and Kit slowly pulled on the door and eased it open. He did so slowly as his eyes took in the widening view of the inside of the cabin as he pulled open the door.

He could hear some voices from the front of the cabin. He carefully closed the back door and then moved forward, walking slowly with his heels coming down first and then his toes.

Kit stopped at the edge of the entrance to the kitchen from a hallway and listened. Now he could hear what was being said. The short gunman was apparently telling others that he had told the two young bikers that the ranger was out on a call and the station was closed until he returned, and they were stuck there with car trouble and were waiting for him to get back.

Kit got to the end of the hall and stopped just short of the opening into the next room. He stood there perfectly still and listened and smelled. After almost five minutes he was sure there were two gunmen and that neither one of them were particularly familiar with good body hygiene. One also smelled like cigarettes.

Kit decided to use the element of surprise. He stepped into the next room with his gun extended in a combat stance and said, "Drop your weapons or you'll die where you stand."

In front of Kit was a very large gunman with his back to Kit and to his right was Swifty sitting on a wood en chair. The smaller thug was standing in front of Swifty and facing Kit. His face was filled with astonishment.

The small man moved to his right and drew his pistol with a speed that amazed Kit. At the same moment, Swifty, hands tied behind him, lunged out of his chair and smashed into the back of the small gunman. Both men stumbled and fell to the floor. The small gunman's pistol went flying out of his hand before he hit the floor.

The large gunman turned toward Kit with a face full of rage, and he took a step toward Kit. Kit knew there was no way he could stop the big man before he was on top of Kit. He did what he had been trained to do. He lowered his aim, and he fired two rounds into the man's pelvic region.

The big man let out a scream and suddenly his legs failed him, and he fell to the floor like a marionette whose strings have been cut.

The sound of Kit's gunfire caused both the small gunman and Swifty to freeze in their places on the floor.

Keeping his gun sighted on the shorter thug, Kit looked over to Swifty.

"You all right, Partner?"

"I'm all right. I'll be better when you cut this rope and get my hands free, so I can choke this little bastard to death."

Kit grinned and with his left hand he pulled out his knife and moved over to where Swifty lay. He knelt down and cut the ropes tying Swifty's hands. The ropes were no sooner free then Swifty bounded to his feet and swiftly moved over and pulled the shorter gunman to his feet by pulling on the man's shirt collar.

"Who the hell are these guys?" asked Kit.

"Well, the big bastard laying there screaming and bleeding on the floor is called Mr. James and this little asshole calls himself Mr. Kellogg.

"Why don't you recycle this rope they used on you and tie up Mr. Kellogg and his partner," said Kit.

"It'll be my pleasure said Swifty and in a few minutes had Mr. Kellogg's hands tied behind his back and then attended to Mr. James as well. Mr. James was in such pain he seemed oblivious to the fact that Swifty was tying his hands behind him.

"Did you see any sign of Nix?"

"I didn't have much time, but now that you mention it, I didn't even hear them mention him either."

"I'll look around," said Kit.

A quick tour of the cabin revealed a loft with a small bedroom and bath and the downstairs was the lobby and office with the kitchen and a small eating area on the main floor.

Kit looked in the bedroom and the office for Nix's satellite phone, but he found nothing, not even the charging station.

When he returned to the lobby, Swifty was in the act of dragging Mr. James out the front door and into the yard next to the cabin. Mr. James was screaming with every step Swifty took. Finally and mercifully, Mr. James passed out.

"I got tired of being cooped up in this cabin and if there are more of these goons out there I want to be able to see them coming this time."

Kit smiled at his partner. "That works for me, too."

Kit then jerked Mr. Kellogg to his feet and escorted him out the front of the cabin and over next to where Mr. James lay still.

Kit walked over to Swifty's truck and came back with a sandwich and a can of pop.

"Did I mention that lunch was ready?" he said to Swifty.

"This is not how I usually choose to work up an appetite, but lunch sounds good."

Swifty devoured the sandwich and then pointed to the prone and still bleeding Mr. James.

"What do we do about treating him?"

"Be my guest," said Kit.

"You shot him. You treat him."

"I don't think he'll bleed to death and I think the pain is as much mental as physical to him."

"We need to get in touch with the sheriff as soon as we can," said Swifty.

"I agree, but I'm not sure how we do that without a satellite phone."

"Did you check our guests for phones?" asked Swifty.

"An oversight on my part," said Kit.

He proceeded to frisk first Mr. Kellogg and then the unconscious Mr. James.

"All these boys have on them is knives, ammo, and cash."

"No I.D.?"

"Not even a scrap piece of paper."

"I think I see the answer to our problem," said Swifty. He pointed to the north where a dust tail rose behind a National Forest Service green pickup slowly making its way south to the Dutch Joe Guard Station.

CHAPTER
TWENTY-FOUR

Sure enough, the pickup slowed and pulled off the dirt road and came to a stop in front of the ranger cabin.

The truck's driver side door opened and out stepped Nix in his ranger uniform. His face registered shock at the scene in front of him

He walked over to where Kit and Swifty were standing and spreading his hands wide, he looked straight at Kit and asked, "What is all this? Who are these people? What happened here?"

"We had a little ruckus, Nix. We brought back two of the gunmen who tried to ambush us up in the mountains and then we got jumped by these two yahoos who were hiding out in your ranger cabin."

Nix pointed to the prone and bleeding Mr. James and asked, "What happened to this poor man?"

"He resisted," said a stone faced Swifty.

"Well, what do we do with all these people?" Nix asked as he took in the two members of the Red Team that were still handcuffed to the horse trailer.

"We need your help to get in touch with the sheriff. This will become his problem as soon as we can get him here," said Kit.

"We looked for your satellite phone, but we couldn't find it," Kit added.

Nix looked around once more as though the totality of what had happened was now slowly dawning on him.

"The satellite phone? Oh yes, the satellite phone. I think I left it in my truck. I'll go get it for you. I think it's charged up, but I'm not sure."

Nix walked back to his pickup truck and opened the driver's side door and began rummaging around behind the seat. Finally he exited the truck, and he stopped as he stood behind the truck door that was between him and the two cowboys. After a pause like he was adjusting his clothing, he walked back toward Kit and Swifty with the satellite phone in his left hand, keeping his right hand against his hip.

As he neared Swifty he stopped and asked, "Which one of you wants the phone?"

"I'll take it," said Kit and he stepped forward to take the satellite phone from Nix's hand.

Instead, Nix dropped the phone on the ground and a 12 gauge pump shotgun swung up from his right hip and now was in his hands covering both Swifty and Kit.

"Nix. What the hell is this?" asked Kit.

"You two will shut your mouths and place your weapons on the ground in front of you. Once you have done that you will take two steps backwards. Do you understand?"

Kit looked at Swifty. He was as surprised as Kit. Swifty nodded at Kit and both of them took out their weapons and placed them on the ground in front of them and then took two steps back.

"Now, both of you get on your knees and put your hands behind your heads."

Both Kit and Swifty went down to their knees and placed their hands behind their heads.

"You mind telling us, just what you think you're doing, Nix?"

Nix smiled in response. Now that he had the two dangerous cowboys disarmed and on the ground, he was less nervous, and felt more in control.

"My name is not Nix. I'm not a forest ranger. I'm a professional thief."

"So you work for one of these treasure hunting outfits we keep running into?" asked Kit.

"Actually I'm an owner of a company that specializes in finding buried treasure all over the world."

"So which one of these gun hands here work for you?" asked Swifty.

"All four of these gentlemen are in my employ, Mr. Swifty. And speaking of that, I will trouble you for your handcuff key."

Swifty nodded and then he slowly took down his right hand and reached into his shirt pocket and came out with a small handcuff key.

"If you will be so kind as to throw the key over to me," said the young gunman.

Swifty carefully tossed the key so that it landed just in front of Nix. He carefully bent over and picked it up with his left hand while holding the shotgun in his right hand.

"What happened to the real Mr. Nix?" asked Kit.

"The real Mr. Nix was having a beer in the bar at the Outlaw Inn in Rock Springs on his way to his new assignment at Dutch Joe's Guard Station when I first made his acquaintance. If I'm not mistaken, he is resting peacefully somewhere in the Red Desert."

"So you took his place."

"Actually I became Mr. Nix. I fooled his supervisor when I arrived and I certainly fooled the two of you.

Both of you still have surprised looks on your faces. Being young, Mr. Nix allowed me to know or find out pretty much everything you two cowboys were doing while you were looking for the crash site."

"You didn't find out about the crash site, did you, whatever your name is?"

"For now you can call me Stone," he said smiling at his little inside joke. "It is both correct and appropriate."

"So what now?" asked Kit.

"First things, first," said Stone.

He moved over and pulled out a short knife, and he cut the bonds of Mr. Kellogg.

"Mr. Kellogg, kindly take this handcuff key and free our two associates from the Red team."

Mr. Kellogg looked up at Stone like he was a ghost or certainly someone he had never seen before.

"That's right, I'm Black One. I'm your boss. Do exactly as I say and you just might get out of here with your hide intact. I am not impressed with your performance or the Red Team's performance."

Kellogg moved over to the horse trailer and after a little trial and error, he succeeded in unlocking the handcuffs binding Snake and Red Two. Soon all three men were standing next to the kneeling cowboys with expectant looks on their faces.

"What do you want us to do?" said an unsure Kellogg.

"I want you to wait until I give you an order and then I want that order carried out to the letter. Do you three morons understand?"

"Yes, sir," replied the three men in unison.

"Mr. Kellogg, please carefully search both of the prisoners."

Kellogg scrambled forward and began to search both Kit and Swifty while they were on their knees.

"Search the packs they were wearing when they walked in as well."

Kellogg searched the packs and came up with empty hands.

"No diamonds?" asked Stone.

"There ain't no diamonds in these packs," replied Kellogg.

Stone turned to face Kit and Swifty. "You two have caused me a great deal of time and money in trying to find the lost diamonds that were carried on that crashed air mail flight."

He looked over at his beaten and ragged men and then back at Kit and Swifty.

"You two have proven to be worthy advisories, but I am tired of playing this game and now I want direct answers as to where I can put my hands on the diamonds. Do I make myself clear?"

Both Kit and Swifty just stared back at Stone.

"I suspected as much. I have discovered just how tough you two are and since I want answers in a hurry, I have decided to use a method that I doubt either of you two cowboys are prepared for."

With that Stone walked back to where he had dropped the satellite phone. He stooped over and picked it up and turned it on. He watched the lighted face of the phone as it began to try to make a connection, and then he smiled as the connected light came on.

He turned his back to Kit and Swifty and said a few words into the phone that they could not hear. Then he turned the phone off and turned around to face them.

"One last time, where are the diamonds?"

All he got from Kit and Swifty was silence and glares.

"Very well, then we will do this the hard way," said Stone.

He turned away from Kit and Swifty and walked over to the front porch of the ranger cabin. He stepped up on the porch and took a seat on the wooden bench and began to look to the north.

Kit looked at Swifty and the look he got back told him Swifty was as clueless as Kit was about what Stone planned to do next.

*   *   *

After a wait of about fifteen minutes, a dust cloud to the north of the ranger station announced the arrival of another vehicle.

As the vehicle approached the ranger cabin, it slowed down and the dust cloud cleared revealing the vehicle to be a dusty black Suburban.

The driver pulled up in front of the cabin and stopped. He stepped out of the Suburban onto the edge of the road. He was a tall skinny man dressed in black fatigues like a SWAT team member would wear. He had on a black baseball cap and he wore gloves and black combat boots. He had pale white skin, dark hair, and a thin mustache.

He moved to the back of the Suburban and opened the passenger door on the driver's side of the vehicle. He stuck his head into the interior and when he emerged he was holding a female who had her arms tied to her body and her hands were bound behind her. She had a gag in her mouth and she wore a dirty white blindfold.

She was wearing a rumpled and dirty ranger uniform.

Kit and Swifty both recognized her as the lady ranger they had met on the trail. Kit seemed to remember that her name was Patricia or Pat. She was the one they were pretty sure was a fake ranger and probably working for one of the treasure hunting companies.

"Bring the lady over here, Mike. Good job in getting here promptly after I called you."

The man Stone had referred to as Mike pulled the stumbling woman roughly forward until he had her standing next to Black One.

"Okay, Mr. Kit and Mr. Swifty. Here's the deal. I ask you where the diamonds are and you tell me and everyone gets to go home safe and sound. I ask you and you do not tell me, I cut off one of this lady's ears. Then I ask again and if you don't tell me where the diamonds are, well I think you get the idea."

"So it is really very simple. You give me what I want or this fairly attractive woman will get a lot less attractive. Do you two understand?"

Both Kit and Swifty returned Stone's stare and neither man made any indication that they were willing to comply with Stone's demands.

"So you two are planning on being tough guys, huh? Let's see how tough you are after I give you just a little sample of what I have planned for this lady."

With that Stone turned to the bound lady captive who was being held tightly by the one called Mike.

Stone pulled a short, narrow knife from a scabbard on his belt and held it up above his head and let the sun catch blade and reflect the light off it.

"Last chance cowboys," said Stone.

There was no response from either Kit or Swifty.

Stone turned and faced the terrified woman and touched the tip of the knife to the bottom edge of her left ear. She attempted to scream and twist away from Stone's touch, but the sound was muffled by the gag in her mouth and Mike was too strong for her. Without warning, Stone dropped the blade down, reversed the edge so it was pointing up and the in one quick motion he slipped the tip of the blade into her nose and ripped it forward, cutting the flesh apart and he stepped back to avoid being hit with her blood.

The woman screamed, and it was clearly audible in spite of the gag. Blood shot out of her nose.

Every one of Stone's men had unconsciously been drawn to the scene in front of them and were focused on the brutality of what they were witnessing.

Kit knew this was probably his only chance to do something and he lunged to his feet and then quickly moved to his left as he knocked down Snake who had been standing closest to him.

Snake went down and his pistol went flying out of his hand. By this time Swifty had followed Kit's lead and he had knocked down Red One.

Both Kellogg and Mike were still shocked by this sudden change of events, and they were slow to react. Kellogg pulled up his pistol, but Snake was in his line of fire, and Mike had his hands full with a screaming and struggling woman.

Kit felt anger greater than any he had ever felt before. He gained his balance and charged forward to grab onto Stone before he could deploy a weapon other than the knife he held in his hand.

Stone was as surprised as his men, but he recovered more quickly and he stepped back, dropped his knife, and reached down to pick up the shotgun he had left on the ground.

As Kit came charging around the falling Snake, Stone got the shotgun to his hip, and he flicked off the safety and pulled the trigger. He was pointing more than aiming, but he had no time for anything else.

The blast hit Kit in the shoulder and tossed Kit's body backwards like he was a rag doll and he fell into a crumpled heap on the ground.

Swifty was in a struggle with Red One and Kellogg when he heard the blast of the shotgun, and he saw Kit hit and knocked down.

"Hold him, don't kill him," yelled Stone.

"We need him alive, don't kill him."

The two men held Swifty securely and then tied his hands behind him and forced him to lie on his belly on the ground. The screaming woman had fallen to the ground where she lay there sobbing and bleeding.

"Sit up, Mr. Swifty. It's time for you to tell us the truth about the location of the diamonds," said Stone.

Swifty was forced to sit up on the ground and Stone and his four men stood around him.

"I won't ask you again, Mr. Swifty. Either you tell me where the diamonds are or I will have Mr. Kellogg here take his pistol and put both the lady and your friend Mr. Kit out of their misery with a bullet to the head. Do you understand me?"

"Boss," said Red One. "Some guy is coming down the road with horses."

Stone and the men turned to look and sure enough they could see a strange sight. Some old codger wearing a derby hat and a St. Louis Cardinal jersey was walking down the road from the south leading three horses and a mule.

Stone recognized the horses as belonging to Swifty and Kit along with their pack horse. He also remembered them telling him about some old geezer prospector that they had run across up on the mountain.

Then a thought crossed his mind. "Maybe the diamonds were in the saddle bags of the horses or on the pack horse. Wouldn't that be a surprise that solved most of his current problems."

Stone and all of his men had stopped where they were standing and turned to stare at the old man leading the three horses. That moment made them all perfect targets.

Suddenly, Snake threw up his hands and his body flew backwards with a red mist following his descent.

Then Red One's head disappeared to be replaced by a bloody, pulpy mess. Mike turned to run and was blown forward in his intended path as blood flew from the exit wound in his chest.

"Sniper," yelled Stone. He and Kellogg ran for the Suburban. Kellogg didn't make it. A bullet almost blew his head off and his headless body bounced off of Stone and plunged to the ground.

Stone was able to get into the Suburban and get the vehicle running. He threw the big truck in gear as a bullet went through the driver's side window and just missed his head as it exited through the passenger side window. Stone smashed the gas pedal to the floor and big machine's tires spun and threw gravel and dirt as they searched for traction. When they found it the big SUV shot forward heading south on the dirt road and leaving a huge plume of dust in its wake.

The old timer and the three horses had disappeared off the road.

Swifty got to his feet with some difficulty as his hands were still tied behind his back. He looked around him in amazement. There were four gunmen dead on the ground. The bleeding woman was lying in a heap and sobbing. Kit was not moving.

Swifty ran over to the pile of personal belongings that Kellogg had left on the ground when he had searched Kit and Swifty and their packs. He found his knife and pulled it free of its scabbard. Then he tried to position the knife in his hands so he could try to saw through the ropes that bound his hands.

"Can I help you there, sonny?"

Swifty looked up to see none other than O.J. Pratt standing next to him. Pratt had tied off the three horses to the front porch of the ranger cabin and had his knife out ready to cut Swifty free.

"You bet," said Swifty.

Swifty turned around so O.J. could easily get at the ropes around his hands and in a few seconds the ropes were cut and Swifty's hands were free.

Swifty then ran over to where Kit lay on the ground, and he carefully rolled him over.

Kit's left shoulder had taken the brunt of the blast and his shirt was ripped and bloody. Swifty checked for a pulse and found it to be steady and fairly strong. He then rolled up his jacket and after holding up Kit's head, he slipped the jacket under him to elevate his head.

Swifty then got up and ran over to his pickup truck to get his first aid kit. When he had retrieved it, he looked up and saw the O.J. had untied the woman's ropes, taken off her blindfold and pulled out her gag. O.J. had taken out a handkerchief and was helping her hold it to her nose to help staunch the flow of blood. He had her partially sitting up and leaning back against his leg for support.

Swifty quickly moved to Kit's side and used his knife to cut away the torn and bloody pieces of his shirt that covered the wounded area of his shoulder. Then he used a cotton swab soaked with rubbing alcohol to carefully and gently clean the wound area. He could see some of the shotgun pellets visible in the wound and he then used another gauze pad to apply pressure to the wound to help stop the bleeding.

Frantic with fear for his best friend, Swifty looked up and said, "What the hell just happened, O.J.?"

"Him over there is what just happened," said O.J. as he pointed toward the road.

Jogging across the road was a tall older man with white hair that was closely cropped under his cowboy hat. He wore a faded denim shirt and worn blue jeans and cowboy boots. He was broad shouldered and he had a thick chest. He moved gracefully like an athlete as he ran toward them. In his right hand was Kit's AR-10 rifle.

As the man got closer, Swifty could see he had about a two-day stubble of grey beard on a face that looked like it had been carved out of rock. His face was lined and had the careworn look of a man who had endured much of what the world had thrown at him and still survived.

The man ignored O.J. and the woman and he didn't even look at Swifty. He ran directly to Kit and knelt at his side. He took off the glove on his right hand and gently stroked the side of Kit's face.

"Jesus Christ. I can't believe this. That son-of-a-bitch shot my son."

Swifty took a closer look at the man. Sure enough, he realized he was looking at a much older version of Kit.

"Do you know where that asshole in the ranger suit was headed, son?"

Swifty was still in shock at finding himself next to Kit's long-lost father. He hesitated for a second and then replied, "He headed south. He has two choices when the road ends at a T-junction. He can go north, but that pins him in because of Jackson and the two parks. He can go south, and that gets him on the Interstate to go east or west."

"Sounds like south is the best bet. Can I intercept him with a horse?"

"Yes sir. You should be able to beat him going overland and intercept him at Buckskin Crossing at the Big Sandy River."

"Show me on the map."

Swifty ran to the truck and returned with a topographical map. He pointed out the best route for a man and a horse to get to Buckskin Crossing.

"Are you Kit's father?"

"I sure as hell am, son. I assume you're his pal, Swifty."

"Yes sir."

"I'm Tom Andrews, Kit's father," said the tall man as he held out his hand."

"I'm thrilled and relieved to meet you, sir. You saved our lives," said Swifty as he found his hand engulfed in the older man's large hand.

"I'm counting on you to help save Kit's life, Swifty."

Tom reached in his pocket and handed Swifty a satellite phone. "I called for Big Dave and some help, but we need medical help. Call the sheriff or 911 or whoever the hell can help us. You call for help and stay with my son. I'll take two horses and keep a fast pace so I can stop that miserable excuse for a human being."

Tom rose, checked briefly with O.J. and the woman and then he mounted one horse and held the reins of the other. He turned his head toward Swifty.

"I'm counting on you, Swifty. Don't let me down."

"I won't let you down. He's my best friend. Don't let that asshole get away with this."

Tom Andrews touched his finger to his hat brim, turned his horse and jabbed his heels into the animal's flanks and the man and two horses were launched over the dirt road and into the brush beyond. Soon, Swifty could not either see or hear them.

CHAPTER
TWENTY-FIVE

Victor Blume's heart was still pounding when he finally decided that he was out of range of the mystery sniper, who had killed all of his men. He began to slow his speed in the black Suburban so he could maintain control and not slide off the dirt road into one of the side ditches.

As he slowed down to a more manageable speed he took the opportunity to take stock of the situation. He checked himself over and could find no wounds or injuries. The only thing he found was the blood of Mr. Kellogg all over the right side of his uniform and on the right side of his face. He slowed the vehicle's speed down even more as he reached over and opened the glove box compartment and found some tissues. He closed the glove box and started to wipe off the side of his face. He looked at the tissues and they were coated with fresh blood and small bits of grey matter were pieces of Kellogg's brain. He had seen the head explode and his only thought then was escape and survival.

Blume tried to piece together what had just happened to him and to his plan. After months of planning and a great deal of expense, the entire deal had blown up with a surprise attack by an unknown sniper.

As he tried to piece together what had just happened, he recalled seeing the old prospector and the three horses on the road to the south of the cabin. It was a perfect set-up he thought. While he and his men were gaping at the old geezer, the sniper had taken them all down. He must have used a semi-automatic weapon and used it well. The sniper had to be a professional. Blume had never seen shooting like that. The sniper had killed four men in less than ten seconds. Blume didn't hear the sound of the first shot until Red One had been blown away.

The longer he drove, the calmer Blume got. Now he had to think about what to do next. He had to plan an escape and then he could worry about what if anything he might salvage from this disaster.

He turned on the vehicle's navigation system, but it was not much help. All it showed was empty road on the small screen. He needed more information.

Blume slowed down and came to a stop. He could see nothing in front of him and nothing in the rear view mirror. There were no other vehicles, people or structures in sight. He opened the console next to him and withdrew a map of Wyoming.

He opened the map and spread it against the steering wheel in front of him. Once he found his approximate location he looked to the east on the map. Blume could see he would be coming to a T-junction. He could go to his right or north and head to Jackson. If he did that he could see that he would be hemmed in by the two national parks. There was no quick way out of the state. There was an airport in Jackson, but by the time he got there, it was likely that law enforcement would have been notified, and he would likely be trapped there.

He needed to use the short time advantage he had to get as far away and to get as invisible as possible. The vehicle was not a problem. There were thousands of black Suburbans in the west and his dusty vehicle wouldn't stand out in a crowd. He had to be careful though. If he tried to stick to back roads he ran the risk of car trouble or running out of gas. He checked the fuel gauge. The tank was only half full. He needed to get to a gas station quickly.

He looked at the map again. If he went south he could take one of two routes and wind up on Interstate 80 in less than two hours. Then he could decide to go either west or east and get out of the state in a relative hurry.

South it was.

*   *   *

Moving at a fast pace over the open but broken terrain between Dutch Joe's Guard Station and Buckskin Crossing was an effort that required full concentration. Still Tom had nagging thoughts of what condition his son was in and how wise he had been to leave him to take up the chase for the man who had shot him.

Tom wasn't interested in justice for the shooter. He had spent too much time on covert operations in places all over the world for his government over the last fifteen years to have even the slightest concern for the shooter's legal rights. The man had shot Tom's son. Tom wanted revenge.

As he rode, Tom reflected on what had just happened. He had been gone from the United States for almost seven years. He had been wounded and captured on a covert mission in an unfriendly country. He had spent almost four years in prison and then escaped, only to be recaptured and imprisoned again. About two years later he had managed to escape again. This time he was able to find refuge with a family friendly to America, and he was nursed back to health in a sparsely settled part of the country. It had taken him almost an entire year to regain his health and his strength and to make his way out of the country he had been captured in. Then using contacts from a previous mission he was able to arrange to be smuggled to Mexico in a tramp steamer. Once in Mexico he had barely avoided getting tossed in a Mexican jail because he lacked proper identification papers, and he ended up slipping across the border into the United States like so many illegal immigrants had before him. Tom had surfaced in El Paso, Texas, and was able to get a call through to his old friend, Woody Harrison.

To his amazement, he discovered his son had somehow ended up in Kemmerer, Wyoming, and became almost a member of Big Dave Carlson's family. He had received new identification papers and funds wired by Woody and then flown to Salt Lake City where Big Dave and Woody had met him and driven him to Kemmerer.

On the trip to Kemmerer, he learned from Harrison that his son and his son's pal Swifty Olson were up in the Wind River Mountains looking for an old plane crash site, the pilot, and a cache of diamonds.

He also learned that Kit and Swifty were dealing with some unsavory treasure hunters, and Tom decided to drive up to the Wind Rivers to have a reunion with the son he had not seen in almost ten years.

When he reached the mountains near Squaw Creek, Tom began searching for his son and ran into the colorful and entertaining O.J. Pratt who told him he had indeed had the pleasure of meeting Tom's son.

O.J. Pratt had also come across Kit and Swifty's horses and pack horse and had them with him when he had run into Tom on the trail. O.J. knew they had a camp at Dutch Joe's Guard Station and they had headed there with the horses. As they were approaching the ranger station, they heard shots and after scouting ahead, Tom realized that things at Dutch Joe's Guard Station had taken a bad turn for his son and Swifty, and he needed to act quickly. Tom had O.J. create a diversion with the horses while he found a good sniper's nest with an excellent view of the ranger cabin and its surroundings.

Tom had used his son's AR-10 which he had found in the scabbard on Kit's horse. It was an excellent weapon and the scope was better than anything he had used while on previous covert missions. Using it on the four gunmen had been both easy and deadly.

Seeing his unarmed son get gunned down by some lunatic outlaw was the worst thing Tom had ever witnessed. He had felt helpless when he saw Kit fall and then he had done his best to take it out on the gunmen standing around the ranger cabin. He regretted that he had not killed them all when he had the chance.

Tom turned his attention to the trail he was on. He stopped and looked at the map and decided he was over half way to his destination at Buckskin Crossing. He changed horses and then he urged his fresh mount to move even faster.

After almost twenty minutes he hit the south bank of the Big Sandy River and there was a well-used game trail parallel to the river. He urged his horse on and increased their speed.

Finally he could see downstream to where a bridge crossed the shallow, but wide Big Sandy River. As he neared the bridge, he could see the remains of a burned out building located down from the road and next to the river.

Tom rode his horse up the bank from the river onto the shoulder of the paved road that crossed the river on the bridge.

Sitting on his horse in the middle of the north end of the bridge Tom realized he would need something to use as a road block. He decided to use the horses. He tied one horse to the rail on the west side of the bridge and the other horse to the rail on the other side of the bridge.

Then Tom stood in the middle of the road and looked to both sides for a good shooting position. He found what he was looking for on the south side of the river on a high rock outcropping that had an unobstructed view that dominated the south approach to the bridge.

Before he could move off the road he heard the engine of an approaching vehicle coming from the north approach to the bridge. Thinking it might be a local rancher, Tom stayed on the bridge to flag them down and let them pass by his horse barricade.

The engine noise got louder and then he was surprised to see a bright yellow and black Jeep Wrangler with Colorado license plates come roaring over the top of the north rise and headed down to the bridge.

Tom stood in the middle of the bridge and was successful in flagging down the Jeep.

The Jeep came to a halt in front of Tom. The Jeep's canvas top was down and he found himself looking directly at the driver, an attractive young blonde woman who looked to be in her mid to late twenties.

The blonde shut off her engine and stood up in the Jeep to face Tom over the top of the Jeep's windshield.

"What's going on, sir?" she asked.

"I'm sorry to bother you ma'am, but I'm setting up a road block for a killer, who I suspect will be here in any minute coming from the South."

"You said killer? Have people been hurt?"

"Yes, they have. I have an injured woman and my son was shot."

"Where are they?"

"I left them back at Dutch Joe's Guard Station southwest of here."

"I can help them. I'm a registered nurse. I'm here in Wyoming on vacation."

Tom looked carefully at her. Her hair was almost white blonde and was pulled back in a pony-tail. She had definite Scandinavian facial features and bright blue eyes. She had a determined look on her face that somehow told Tom she was someone he could trust.

He gave her directions to Dutch Joe's Guard Station and showed it to her on his map.

"I can find that easily. Will I run into this killer if he's coming from there?"

"Most likely you will. Just don't stop or get tangled up with him. I need you to help my son. And please be careful."

"I'm a big girl and I can take care of myself. What's your son's name?"

"His name is Kit. Kit Andrews."

"Kit, like in Kit Carson?"

"That would be correct, Miss."

The blonde smiled and fired up her Jeep and shot down the road.

Tom watched her disappear over the next rise to the south, and then he began jogging to the spot in the rocks he had picked out.

Tom did not have long to wait. In about fifteen minutes he heard the sound of a car engine coming from the south. Very shortly he could see the dust plume that the speeding vehicle was making. He remembered that when he was a kid they referred to such a dust plume as a "rooster tail."

The approach to the south end of the bridge was more gradual than the one from the north and it would give Tom more time to take his shot.

He decided to shoot out the front tires of the Suburban before it got very close to the end of the bridge and his horse barricade.

*   *   *

Blume had increased his speed as he grew more comfortable with the gravel road. He was driving between forty-five and fifty miles an hour and the road was well maintained and fairly smooth for a gravel road. There were lots of curves and he had to be careful that he didn't start to slide on the gravel. He had only seen three vehicles on the road since he had taken the south fork. Two ranch pickups and a yellow Jeep did not account for much traffic and that was fine with him.

As he drove over a rise, the road curved down and to the right. He could see a wide, but shallow river ahead of him with a metal bridge crossing over the water. A second look told him that something was wrong as he could see what looked like horses on the bridge.

"What idiot would tie up horses on a bridge on a public road?"

The next thing he knew his right front tire had blown out, and as he tried to turn into the slide, the left front tire blew out as well. Blume lost control of the heavy black Suburban, and it slid off the road into the ditch on the left side and when it hit the far edge of the ditch, the vehicle rolled over and slid on its top until it was about twenty yards from the edge of the river.

Blume felt the airbags deploy and he was slammed back against his seat with alarming speed and force that caused him to black out.

When Blume regained consciousness, he was upside down in the overturned vehicle, hanging by his seat belt.

As he turned his head to the driver's side window he could see a large pair of cowboy boots. He didn't remember seeing anyone before the crash. Had someone come along and found him. Maybe some rancher?

The next thing he knew someone had cut or released the seat belt and he had crashed head first into the roof of the Suburban. Then a pair of hands came through the window and he felt himself dragged headfirst through the window and out onto the rough ground. He was having trouble with his vision, but he could hear the sound of the water moving in the river next to him.

Before his head had cleared, Blume found himself being jerked to his feet and slammed back against the upside down body of the Suburban.

He looked up to see an older cowboy with a stern face that looked like it was made out of granite and eyes that were full of nothing but hate.

Blume felt fear spread throughout his body. He was a man who enjoyed inflicting fear and pain on others. He, in fact, had a low pain threshold and as he stood there he could feel his bladder empty seemingly of its own accord.

"You sniveling piece of dog shit. I should do the world a favor and stuff you back in this truck set it on fire and have you burn up with it."

"Oh, please mister. Don't hurt me. Please don't hurt me. I'll make it right by you. I've got money. I've got lots of money. Name your price."

"You can't buy me, sonny. You fucked with the wrong family.

"Look. If you're a cop, you have to obey the law. You have to take me into custody. You can't hurt me. It's against the law."

"Unfortunately for you I ain't no cop. I'm a pissed off father of a son that you shot when he was unarmed."

"Kit is your son?"

"One and the same."

"I thought you were dead Mr. Andrews."

"Not hardly."

"I'm sorry for what I did. Please don't hurt me."

"You should have thought about that a lot sooner, you cowardly asshole."

With that Tom raised his pistol and shot Blume in the right knee.

Blume screamed and fell to the ground clutching at his now torn and bloody knee.

"Oh, my God. You shot me. You shot me. Why in God's name did you shoot me?"

"You were trying to escape, asshole."

Blume was sobbing and as he held his injured right knee with both hands he stretched his left leg out in front of him.

Tom fired again, shooting Blume in the left knee.

Blume screamed and rolled over on the ground in pain and anguish.

"You son-of-a-bitch, why did you shoot me again?" Blume screamed!

"You tried to escape twice."

*   *   *

An hour later, Tom had stopped the bleeding and bandaged up Blume's knees. He had slung Blume over the saddle of his second horse. He had Blume's hands tied to one stirrup and his feet tied to the other stirrup and had strapped him to the saddle for good measure.

After checking everything for good knots and proper tightness, Ted swung into the saddle. He headed north on the road leading the second horse with Blume as an unwilling cargo, he jabbed his horse in the flanks with his heels. It had been a long time since he had been in the saddle and this time it felt both natural and right.

CHAPTER
TWENTY-SIX

Tom hadn't ridden more than two miles when he met a rancher in a pickup truck who stopped to see what was going on. When Tom explained what had happened, the rancher had left in a cloud of dust only to return with his pickup truck towing a horse trailer.

Soon Tom was sitting in the passenger seat of the rancher's pickup truck listening to the man talking about his cattle ranch and how tough things were in the market this year. Within minutes, Tom was sound asleep.

*   *   *

Swifty kept looking at his watch while he knelt next to his best friend. He had already changed the gauze bandage on Kit's shoulder twice as they had become soaked with blood. Finally, the bleeding seemed to have almost stopped.

Swifty looked up and to the south along the dirt roadway.

"Where the hell was the help he had called for? He knew Big Dave and Woody were moving heaven and earth to get help to Kit, but they were pretty far away from Dutch Joe's Guard Station. Where the hell was the sheriff? His friend could be dying here in the middle of nowhere just because there was no help available close by.

Swifty looked over at where O.J. Pratt had cleaned and bandaged Patricia's damaged nose. O.J. had her sitting on the bench on the porch of the ranger cabin, and he was holding her hand and talking softly to her to keep her as calm as possible.

Swifty was angry. He felt helpless. He felt he had failed Kit and not done enough when they had made their move to turn the tables on their captors. He felt stupid for allowing the man who had portrayed himself as Nix to completely fool him.

Suddenly, Swifty saw the rise of a dust rooster tail coming hell bent for leather from the south. As the vehicle got closer he was disappointed to see that it was not a sheriff's vehicle, but a bright yellow and black Jeep Wrangler.

As the Jeep approached the ranger cabin the driver slammed on the brakes and slid sideways on the dirt road for about thirty yards and then the driver straightened the Jeep out and roared off the road and onto the grass near where Swifty's pickup truck and horse trailer were parked, and then slid to a stop.

Swifty was shocked to see the driver leap out of the Jeep with a small bag in her hand. He had a hard time believing his eyes. A gorgeous blond woman was running toward him and yelling something.

"Where's Kit? Where's Kit?" The young woman was repeating and Swifty stood and pointed down to his prone friend.

The women came up to Swifty and immediately went to her knees and began to examine Kit. She peppered Swifty with questions while she opened her bag and began taking items out of it.

She looked at Swifty's shocked face and said slowly, "I'm Shirley. I'm a registered nurse. Kit's father sent me."

Swifty came out of his temporary state of shock and answered each of her questions, and then asked how he could help.

"You did a good job of cleaning the wound and stopping the bleeding," said Shirley.

"I did the best I could. Kit's my best friend."

"A best friend is a good thing to have when someone shoots you in the shoulder," said Shirley with a smile and a twinkle in her bright blue eyes.

"Hand me that bottle and those tweezers by the handle. Don't touch the ends!"

"No ma'am. I mean yes ma'am," said a befuddled Swifty.

Shirley worked quickly and after cleaning the wound again, she was able to remove many of the shotgun pellets with the medical tweezers. When she was done she cleaned the wound again and then sprinkled a powdered sulfa drug on the open wound and then put a clean bandage on it. She was careful to tape the bandage in place so it wouldn't move.

"He was very lucky," said Shirley.

"What do you mean, lucky?"

"Usually when someone shoots you with a 12 gauge shotgun, they load it with double ought buckshot. I could be mistaken, but these pellets look like they are about a 7 ½ load."

"You know about shotgun loads?" asked a surprised Swifty.

"I grew up on a ranch in Colorado. I had three brothers. Some months we ate what we killed. I learned to shoot my share."

Swifty looked at her like she was speaking a language he had never heard before.

"He was also lucky because these pellets are copper coated rather than being straight lead. There's less chance of infection problems."

Swifty just shook his head in amazement.

*　　*　　*

Kit woke up and his vision was blurred and his head felt fuzzy. He felt a lot of pain from his shoulder.

As his vision cleared, he saw a beautiful blond young woman leaning over him. She was staring down at him, and she had a smile on her face.

"Where am I," Kit moaned. He closed his eyes and opened them again. She was still there.

"Am I dead? Are you an angel? Am I in heaven?"

"Well, you're in Wyoming and that's pretty close to heaven in my book," the angel replied.

Kit looked at those bright blue eyes with a twinkle in them and he found himself at a loss for words.

"Hey Swifty, look south. Help is acoming," yelled O.J. Pratt.

Sure enough a small caravan of sheriff's vehicles and an ambulance were coming down the dirt road from the south with red, white and blue lights flashing. The result looked like something out of a Fourth of July celebration on wheels.

CHAPTER
TWENTY-SEVEN

In the next forty-five minutes Tom and the rancher also arrived at the ranger cabin. The medics from the ambulance wanted to get Kit to a hospital as soon as possible and were arguing with one of Sheriff Hunt's deputies about delaying any questioning of Kit when the matter was quickly settled for them.

A new noise engulfed the area around Dutch Joe's Guard Station when a helicopter appeared on the horizon and quickly managed to land on an open space of ground across the dirt road from the ranger cabin.

The sliding door on the helicopter opened and out stepped a giant of a man wearing a cowboy hat. Big Dave Carlson had arrived.

Big Dave strode over to where Kit was laying and he stopped to announce to no one in particular and everyone in general that he was taking Kit to the hospital in Jackson and no one should be stupid enough to get in his way.

As the medics were loading Kit into the helicopter on a stretcher, Tom took Swifty and Shirley aside.

"I can't thank you enough for helping to save my son's life, Shirley."

"I am glad I happened along and I was glad I could help."

"I was wondering if you might be willing to help a little more."

"What do you have in mind, Mr. Andrews?"

"I'm going on the helicopter with Kit and I'd like you to ride along."

"But what about my Jeep?"

"I think Swifty here can manage to get your Jeep safely up to Jackson."

"You bet. I'd be happy to."

"Will you come? It would mean a lot to me. I almost lost a son today that I hadn't seen in almost ten years."

"It's a deal. I always wanted to see Jackson Hole," said a smiling Shirley.

Minutes later the helicopter was lifting off and heading northwest to Jackson.

Kit was awake and Tom had Shirley take the seat next to Kit's stretcher.

"So you're the nurse who magically appeared to help me?" said Kit.

"Yes, I guess I am."

"So what's your name. I never got to thank you properly."

"My name is Shirley Townsend. I'm a registered nurse."

"Are you from around here, Mrs. Townsend?"

"It's Miss Townsend. I'm not married, and I'm not from around here.

"Ooh," said Kit with a sly smile.

"Where do you live, Miss Shirley Townsend?"

"I live in Boulder, Colorado," said the beautiful nurse with the bright blue twinkling eyes. "Maybe you've heard of it?"

CHAPTER
TWENTY-EIGHT

Two months later Swifty and Kit found themselves sitting in Woody Harrison's law office in Kemmerer. After a short wait, they were joined by Woody, Big Dave and Tom Andrews.

"Gentlemen, I'd like to keep this meeting short and sweet," said Woody.

"That'll be the first goddamn time," said Big Dave.

Woody ignored the jab from his longtime friend and took out a folder from his desk and opened it.

"I thought we needed to clear up a few loose ends that resulted from you boys' recent adventure in the Wind River Mountains."

"Adventure! More like a goddamn chapter out of World War Two," said Big Dave.

"I am happy to announce that after the sheriff's criminal investigation you two boys are cleared of any and all possible charges from the incidents that took place in the Wind River Mountains and around Dutch Joe Guard Station."

Woody turned and looked across his desk at Tom Andrews.

"Tom, I am also happy to report there are no charges against you for the wounds suffered by Mr. Blume who was trying to escape from you."

"Twice," said Big Dave with a smile on his face.

"If I remember correctly the original purpose of this ill-fated expedition was to try to locate the remains of one William Hopper.

"We determined that the original two women who claimed to be his heirs were frauds. I was able to get the help of the Forest Service to assist in removing Mr. Hopper's remains and allowing us to land a helicopter in the Wind River Mountains wilderness area to accomplish that. Since then I have been able to locate Mr. Hopper's living heirs and to notify them of the recovery of his remains.

Unfortunately his heirs are rather poor and unable to pay to have his remains shipped home to Massachusetts, let alone to actually bury him. Using some political assistance I was able to embarrass the United States Postal Service to come up with the money to have the remains moved and to have them properly buried."

Woody paused and looked up at the men seated around him.

"Now would be a good time for a short round of applause," said Woody.

"The boys did a good thing, but the rest of your report is the usual horseshit," said Big Dave.

Woody looked at Big Dave and frowned and then returned to his file.

"As you may remember, we took the coordinates from Kit's GPS and I had Big Dave go up the mountain and retrieve the two bags of diamonds where Kit buried them under the fire pit in the cave. I had him do this before we notified the authorities about the discovery of Mr. Hopper's remains and their exact location which was also on Kit's GPS."

"You can't trust any of those government bastards," said Big Dave.

"After a rather detailed legal wrangle, it was determined that the legal owner of the diamonds is the Diamond Exchange in San Francisco, California who I discovered, are still in business."

Woody paused again, but Big Dave kept quiet this time.

"The Diamond Exchange was thrilled, to say the least, to have the diamonds returned to them. I am happy to say that in appreciation for having the diamonds returned they have forwarded me a cashier's check for the sum of thirty thousand dollars."

"Cheap bastards," snarled Big Dave.

"David, they didn't have to give us anything."

"Screw them and the horse they rode in on," said Big Dave.

"The reason I asked all of you to come here today is to decide what to do with the money."

"You coulda told us that in two minutes. What is it with you goddamn lawyers. Is it because you charge by the word that you use fifty words when six would be enough," said Big Dave.

Woody just leaned his head back and rolled his eyes at the ceiling.

"How about we give ten thousand to Mr. Hopper's heirs for a nice memorial," said Big Dave.

"I'd like to give ten thousand to O.J. Pratt for all his help," offered Kit.

"Plus a case of the whiskey of his choice. We already owe him that," said Swifty.

"That leaves ten thousand. I think that should be split between Kit and Swifty. Any objections?"

"I don't really need the money so I vote we give the ten thousand to Swifty," said Kit.

"Any objections? None noted," said Woody.

"Done and approved and meeting adjourned. All this yakking has made my throat parched and dry. Can a man get a drink around here," said Big Dave.

"Of course he can," said Woody as he reached into a desk drawer and came out with a bottle of good Tennessee Bourbon and five glasses.

While Woody was pouring drinks for everyone, Tom turned to his son and said, "You got any immediate plans son?"

Kit looked up at his father and said, "I'm planning to take a trip down to Boulder, Colorado. I hear it's a real pretty place."

"I wouldn't wait too long to make that trip," said his father with a grin.

Big Dave stood up and reached into his shirt pocket. He took something out of the pocket and then lobbed it in the air to Kit who caught in in his right hand.

"If you're headed to Boulder to see that nurse you shouldn't go empty handed" said Big Dave.

Kit opened his hand and looked down to see a single perfect diamond that immediately caught and reflected light from every source in the room until it looked like the gem in his hand was on fire.

THE END

ACKNOWLEDGEMENT

This novel is a work of fiction that was inspired by my discovery of an old news article about the United States Postal Service Air Mail. The government did get out of the air mail business in 1928 and that was the start of commercial airline service which was created to bid for air mail contracts.

There actually was a pilot nicknamed Wild Bill who crashed his airplane in the Appalachian mountains in 1928. The ten pounds of diamonds he was carrying were never found.

My thanks to my friend Kerry Wong and my long-suffering wife, Nancy L. Callis for their tireless work in proof reading my work and offering politically correct suggestions on editing.

This is the third novel in a series about some mythical people who live only in my imagination. I enjoy bringing them to life and having them act out the stories I have created.

I would also like to thank O.J. Pratt of Pacific Auction in Longmont, Colorado, a master auctioneer from a family of auctioneers for his advice and allowing me to use his name in the novel.

The best reward in writing is in hearing from readers who like what you write. I am always open to comments and suggestions from my readers at rwcallis@aol.com

I am currently doing research for a fourth book about Kit and Swifty.